BARBARA'S SHORTS

AN ECLECTIC MIX OF 32 SHORT STORIES

BARBARA BURGESS

CROWFOOT PUBLISHING

Barbara Burgess
Author
Songwriter
Psychic Medium
www.barbaraburgess.co.uk

GENERAL INFORMATION

Copyright © Barbara Burgess 2021

No part of this publication may be reproduced or transmitted in any form or future form or by any means or future means, including electronic, mechanical, photocopying, recording, or any other information storage or retrieval system without permission, in writing, of the author, apart from any permitted use under U K copyright law.

Please contact the author, Barbara Burgess via her website www.barbaraburgess.co.uk for written permission of use. Or email: hello@barbaraburgess.co.uk

By not obtaining written permission you are committing theft of the author's intellectual property.

Other information

This publication is all my own work.
There may be errors both typographical and grammatical.
The stories in this book are works of fiction.
All stories in this book are made up stories.

All stories in this book are from my own imagination.

Names, characters, businesses, events, and incidents are products of the author's imagination.

Any resemblance to actual persons, living or dead, or actual events is purely coincidental.

SPREAD THE WORD

Please support Barbara in the following:
 *Leave a review on Amazon
 *Give a copy of her book to loved ones, family and friends.
 *Randomly leave a copy of her book in a place where someone else can find it - a seat in the park - a table in a cafe. Random acts of kindness go a long way and are reciprocal.
 *Share her books and details with others:
 www.barbaraburgess.co.uk

For my Family. I love you with all my heart.

"What you do today can improve all your tomorrows." ~ Ralph Marston

CONTENTS

1. Another Us	15
2. A New Life Down Under	20
3. Haunted Weekends At Dranoon Castle	26
4. I Am The Champion	32
5. Brian's Big Day	37
6. Tracy's Halloween Party	43
7. Good Riddance	48
8. Charing Cross	56
9. The Ghost Who Couldn't Frighten People	62
10. James' First Year	71
11. Em And The Blue Fairy	76
12. Flying South	83
13. Boogie Woogie Bugle Boy of Company B	89
Untitled	95
14. Meg To The Rescue	96
15. Sharla	101
16. Harry's Hell Hole	107
17. It's Win, Win	113
18. Dying Wish	119
19. Still Waiting	127
20. The Tigers	133
21. Kevin	138
22. Grandad's New Toy	145
23. Nan To The Rescue	150
Untitled	155
24. What Not To Do With Olive Oil	156
25. Missing, Presumed Dead	161
26. Here Come The Scones	170
27. April Fool's Day	178
28. The Puddle Dippers	186
29. Going Solo	197
30. Beggars Can't Be Choosers	204

31. Laura's Long Distance Lorries	210
32. The Nun's Story	215
About the Author	221
Also by Barbara Burgess	223
Songwriting	225
Barbara's Personal and Professional Qualifications	229
Contact	231

1
ANOTHER US

Mike let a handful of sand slide through his fingers. He stared at Josie. She hadn't changed a bit. It was five years since they'd had that awful row. He couldn't even remember what the argument was about. All he remembered was Josie storming off and then sending him a text to say it was over between them. Now, quite by accident they were together on their favourite stretch of beach on the anniversary of their breakup.

Josie looked straight ahead. She loved to hear the seagulls and watch the waves crashing on the shore.

"Do you remember how we used to walk on top of the cliffs?" Mike said as he raised his arm and pointed to his left.

Josie glanced toward the high white cliffs as memories stirred inside her.

You never, ever held my hand and always walked a few paces ahead of me. I was scared stiff when you got too close to the cliff edge. She thought.

"I'd run ahead of you and take photos of the wind blowing

your hair in your eyes. You always looked so serious. Maybe it was the cold wind up there on the cliffs."

You always looked like an idiot and people thought you were going to either jump off or fall off. No wonder I looked serious. You'd take me up there no matter what the weather and never listened to me when I said I was cold and wanted to get back into the car. She thought.

Mike picked up some more sand and a handful of pebbles and began making an image of a flower in the sand. "What about that time I bought you a massive bunch of red roses for your birthday. We had to go out and buy three vases to put them in because you did not have any big enough."

My birthday was the day before. You forgot my birthday and you forgot to turn up for our dinner date. I had to make up some excuse about us both being sick and cancel the table. You only remembered my birthday after seeing all my cards on the windowsill. Jenny was deep in thought.

"Would you like an ice-cream Josie? Shall I go and get you one? Your favourite is the strawberry isn't it? I won't be long." Said Mike as he fiddled with the change in his trouser pocket.

My favourite ice-cream is raspberry ripple actually, and I love candy floss. Jenny thought.

"Here you are Josie. You'd better take it quick as it's dripping down the cone. I've bought us both some candy floss too. I thought you might like it. A reminder of the good old days."

"Thanks Mike. Yes, I do love candy-floss. How's your Mum these days? I miss our little chats. Sorry to hear about your dad. Your friend David told me he'd passed away but I didn't have an address or phone number for you so I couldn't let you know how sorry I was."

"Oh, that's all right. Water under the bridge now Josie. Mum's fine. Well, sort of. Yes, we all miss dad. Mum has asked about you a few times. But like you say we lost touch. I changed my mobile and you must have too because I did try to get hold of you."

"Yes, I did change it and I live with a group of girls now in a house that's been turned into flats."

"Sounds nice. I moved back in with mum, but you wouldn't have known that anyway. Strange us meeting up here like this. I thought it was you as I passed by the pier and then as I got closer, I realised it was you. Hope I didn't startle you too much when I called out your name." Said Mike.

"No, you didn't startle me. I could hardly hear you though above the sound of the waves crashing and the seagulls overhead. Good job you came over or we would have missed each other." Said Josie.

"Yes," said Mike as he sat on the sand beside Josi.

I wish he'd put his arm around me, I miss his touch. Thought Josie.

"Are you doing anything this evening?" Said Mike.

"Nothing really. The girls often go out on a Saturday. I sometimes go with them. I might tonight if I feel like it. But then, again, I might not. It all depends on how I feel really."

"What are you doing this evening Mike?"

"Oh, I'll probably sit in the hotel. I'm staying at The Grand. They have a pianist in the bar most nights. I'll sit and listen to the music and then probably have an early night. I've got to get back to mum in the morning. I just came down for a couple of nights. To get away from it all you see. I do quite a bit for mum these days and it can be rather tiring. I just needed a break and thought the fresh sea air would do me good. Then I saw you." Said Mike

"Yes, strange that. I don't often come to the beach on my own and especially at weekends when it can get rather crowded." Said Josie.

"Do you remember that row we had Josie?"

"Not really."

How could I forget it? She thought.

"I don't even recall what it was about now Josie. Do you?"

"No, I don't. I don't recall what we argued over." Said Josie.

I caught you snogging with Amanda at the party. You won't remember you were too drunk. Amanda had been after you for weeks and you couldn't keep your hands of her. Jenny's face flushed a little as she remembered that dreadful night.

"Do you ever hear from your friend Amanda at all? I heard from David that you had had a big fallout with her. Is that true? She's quite a nice girl and I thought she was your best friend." Said Mike.

"She was" Said Josie. "But she isn't any more."

"Oh, shame that. Such a good-looking girl too."

Yes, I bet in your eyes she was better looking than me and she had bigger boobs than mine too. Thought Josie.

"She was quite shapely too, If my mind still serves me well, Josie." Said Mike.

"Yes, she was quite shapely. She took up modelling you know." Said Josie.

"Oh Wow," Said Mike. "Look, would you like to spend the evening with me back at the hotel. We can have a meal and listen to the pianist if you like or take a walk along the promenade together. It'll be just like old days." Said Mike.

"No, I don't think so Mike. Thanks for asking. I'll probably just stay in and have my usual pizza and watch a film. The girls will probably be there and they're good company." Said Josie.

"But I thought." Said Mike.

"You thought what, Mike?" said Josie.

"I thought that maybe we could begin where we left off. I

thought we could get back together again. I thought this was not a coincidence but was meant to be, Josie."

"No Mike. What you've been thinking about isn't going to happen. What you remember is another you, another me, another us."

2

A NEW LIFE DOWN UNDER

Joe sat at his mother's dinner table poking his dinner with his fork. Jessica put her hand under the table and gave his knee a reassuring squeeze. They both looked at each other.

"Joe, are you coming down sick with something? You've hardly touched your Sunday Lunch. Jessica has nearly eaten all hers."

"Go, on Joe, tell your Mum." Said Jessica.

"Tell me what, Joe?"

"Well, Mum, I was going to talk to you a while back but could not find the right time to do it."

"What is it Joe?"

"Jessica and I are getting married."

"What, after five years of living together? That's fantastic Joe. Isn't that wonderful, Arthur? Come on, say something Arthur."

"Yes, Mary," said Arthur, "I think that's great. You're not pregnant are you Jessica?"

Jessica laughed, "No Mr. Thorpe, I'm not pregnant."

"Then I can't see the need to get married as you both look very happy as you are."

"Well, it's like this, Dad. We've decided to move to Australia. We've both got jobs to go to and a home waiting for us, but we need to be married. We're actually planning on getting married when we reach Australia."

The colour drained from Arthur's face as his jaw dropped.

"You're what?" said Mary. "You're getting married in Australia? Well, how on earth can your dad and I watch you get married if you're miles away?"

"It's okay Mum, we were hoping you and Dad would come out there to our wedding and visit our new home."

Arthur's hands began to tremble as he stood up forcing his chair to collide with the coffee table, which sent a vase of flowers crashing to the floor.

"Arthur, what on earth are you doing? Look at that mess you've made." Said Mary.

"Not such a mess as I'll make of his face when I get hold of him." Said Arthur, his cheeks now flushed with rage.

"Now don't be like that Arthur, the boy's entitled to live his own life."

"And what about my life?" Said Arthur. "I've spent an entire life-time building up the family business and now he wants to go and throw it all away for some thin-brained idea of a better life in another country. How ungrateful can you get?"

"Dad! It's not like that. It's not like that at all. Jessica and I want our own lives. We've both got our own interests. You know I've never been any good with my hands and building other people's kitchens."

"No, but you can try. All you ever think about is yourself and your dumb ideas of sitting on your arse and working computers."

"Oh Arthur, leave the boy alone. You know he's good at computers and he's got a high-flying job. He never did like working with his hands, as he says. He uses his brain."

"Oh, and I don't. I can see you're on his side. Well, the lot of you can go to hell. I want nothing more to do with any of you." Said Arthur as he slammed the dining room door and stomped into the kitchen followed by a tutting Mary."

"Come on Jessica, we might as well go home. I'm not going to sit here and listen to those two arguing about me in the kitchen. Now you can see why I left home so young and why I was so keen for us to move in together." Said Joe.

"Wait, Joe. We need to make peace with them. No doubt it's been a bit of a shock. We should have told them sooner and not just blurted it all out over Sunday lunch." Said Jessica.

"Oh, so it's all my fault now is it?" said Joe.

"No, it's not your fault and I didn't mean that. I just want you and your dad to get on, that's all." Said Jessica.

"Well, I don't think we'll ever get on. We never have and we never will. Dad could never bear it if I didn't step into his shoes and carry on the family business. I hate kitchens and working with them and I cannot stand working with Dad either, we just don't get on and that's that." Said Joe.

"I think it best if we leave things to settle Joe. Let's tidy up and go home." Said Jessica.

"I guess you're right. I've really gone off my dinner now anyway."

Joe and Jessica began to stack the plates and tidy up the dining room table. Jessica picked the flowers up off the floor while Joe gathered the broken pieces of glass onto a plate and took them out to the dustbin via the front door. As Joe passed the kitchen window the sight of his father, head in hands, being cuddled by his mother only made him feel even more angry than before.

Once, back inside he said, "Come on Jessica, we're definitely going home. Dad will never come around to my way of thinking. All he ever wanted was for me to inherit the family business. I've never been interested in building things. I'm a techie and always have been. I love working with computers, I love my job." Said Joe.

"Yes, Joe, I know. Stop fussing about it. I'm sure they'll come around sooner or later," said Jessica.

"Well, it had better be sooner rather than later," said Joe, "We're going to Australia and that's that."

Joe stepped out into hallway and took his coat from the hook, then helped Jessica on with hers."

"Bye, Mum. Thanks for the dinner, it was lovely. Sorry, but we've got to go now. I'll phone you both tomorrow. Bye Dad."

Not a sound came from behind the closed kitchen door.

"Can you drive back Jessica? I don't feel much up to it. I'll probably do it all wrong. I do everything wrong." Said Joe.

"No, you don't," Said Jessica as she turned on the ignition. "Look your parents will come around to our way of thinking in next to no time. I'm sure of it."

"Well, I just hope you're right, that's all." Said Joe as he rubbed his face with his hands. "We've still got a lot of planning to do and I'm not letting *him* change my mind."

Jessica could see how angry Joe was getting and was glad she was the one driving. No need for any more accidents today.

***

The following day Joe heard nothing from his parents, no phone calls, nothing. Each time he looked at his phone seething anger rose within him once more. His head was filled with arguments with his dad about why he should be going to Australia and why he wanted nothing to do with the family business.

***

A week had gone by and there was still no word from either parent. No-one was going to give in.

"Why don't you answer your phone Joe? Your mum has been ringing you all afternoon." Said Jessica.

"Because I don't want to argue, that's why." Said Joe.

"Maybe it's important, she must have rung at least six times." Said Jessica as she picked up Joe's phone and pointed it at him.

Joe hesitantly took the phone and stood staring at it. Then it rang again.

"Yes Mum." Said Joe.

"Joe, thank goodness you've answered at last." Said Mary.

"What's up Mum? You and Dad changed your minds at last?" Said Joe.

"No, Joe. Your Dad has been taken very poorly." Mary could hardly get the words out. "He passed away a few minutes ago from a heart attack. I'm at the hospital now."

Joe slumped down to the floor and dropped his phone in his lap.

"What's up Joe?" Said Jessica.

"Dad's died. Mum's at the hospital with him now." Said Joe as he wiped tears from his face.

Jessica took the phone and spoke to Mary, "Shall we come over?"

"No, that's all right. I've got everything sorted and my neighbour is very kindly helping me. Tell Joe I love him and I'm okay about the pair of you getting married and leaving me here alone and going to Australia. Bye." The phone went dead.

"You're Mum doesn't need us at the hospital Joe, and she gives you her blessing about Australia." Said Jessica.

Joe placed his head in his hands and sobbed while Jessica sat on the floor beside him, her arm around his shoulder.

***

Three weeks later Joe and Jessica were at the airport with their luggage when Joe heard a quiet voice behind him call his name.

"Joe, Joe."

He turned around.

"Mum, Mum."

"I've come to see you off Joe. I really couldn't let you both go without making amends. I'm sorry if your dad took it so badly but the family business was his life." Said Mary.

"I know," said Joe, "But I just hate kitchens."

Mary chuckled, "I know you do son. So, do I, to tell you the truth. I certainly don't like the one your dad fitted in our house. How can anyone live with purple kitchen cupboards all the time?"

Joe burst out laughing and hugged his mother.

"I'm sorry Mum but we really must go and get our flight now. I'll phone you as soon as we arrive and get the wedding date set and I'll pay for you to come out and visit us."

"Oh, Joe, that will be lovely. I'm so looking forward to it. Now be off you two adventurers and enjoy life down under.

Mary blew Joe and Jessica a kiss as they took the escalator for their flight to their new married life in Australia.

A month later Mary was on her way to their wedding. She held a little keepsake in her hand. A small prayer book with a red rose from Arthur's funeral wreath pressed inside it.

3

HAUNTED WEEKENDS AT DRANOON CASTLE

*I*t had been twenty-four years since she'd last seen it, but the place looked exactly the same, even though she'd only been six at the time. The image of the four tall turrets with a full moon above them and a sky full of stars had stayed in her memory all these years. She'd often dreamed of Dranoon Castle but never thought one day it would be hers. Now with all her relatives dead it was up to Sheila to make something of this dilapidated building.

As she turned the last corner in her new Mercedes, she stopped the car, switched off the engine and stepped onto the narrow lane. It took only a couple of steps, and the magnificent building came into view. She'd chosen to come back this night of the Scorpio Full Moon and had prayed for a clear sky so that she could get some good photographs for advertising purposes.

Sheila lifted the boot of the car, took out the tripod and her camera, set it all up and waited.

Dranoon Castle looked mysterious, lit by the full moon behind it. She waited for some eery-looking clouds to pass over head and then snapped away with her camera. A few bats obliged and made the images look even more spooky. She couldn't wait to get inside, onto her computer and her new website - *Haunted Weekends at Dranoon Castle*

***

Mary and Jim, the resident housekeeper and gardener stood at the top of the stone steps as Sheila approached through the long, sweeping drive.

"It's lovely to see you at last, Miss Sheila." Said Mary as she walked forward with outstretched hand.

"Pleased to meet you both as well."

"I'll get your luggage." Said Jim as he reached inside the boot of the car.

Sheila stepped into the big hallway and stood in awe of the tall ceiling and giant chandelier; paintings of her ancestors hung on the four walls.

"Can we have a meeting in about half an hour, please? I want to explain to you both what I am going to do with this place.

Mary and Jim looked at each other and then nodded at Sheila. Jim carried the baggage up the winding, oak staircase.

***

"Do come in and sit down," said Sheila as she beckoned Mary

and Jim over to the marble fireplace with its pile of red-glowing logs in the grate.

"I've got to make a living from this place, as I'm sure you must realise."

Mary and Jim nodded but looked puzzled.

"I've decided to do haunted weekends and ghost hunts. Now,

I know this place isn't haunted but that is the least of my worries."

Jim put his hand to his mouth to cover a cough while Mary nudged him in the ribs with her elbow.

"I've got some really good ideas for a website and I need to know which rooms are the best for letting out for a weekend at a time. We can begin with one or two rooms as we get all the others re-decorated. Mary, to begin with we will have to do the food and all the hard work ourselves until I can afford to employ more staff. Jim you will have to do your best to keep the approach to the house spic and span and any maintenance work that needs doing. Any questions?

Mary and Jim both looked pale and shook their heads.

"Now I'm going to get on with developing my website tonight so that we can get some bookings. Mary you can show me around the house tomorrow and would you mind bringing a nice supper to my room in about an hour's time."

Mary nodded and then followed Jim out of the study.

Sheila began climbing the stairs to her room but was startled by someone calling her name. She turned around, thinking it was Mary but there was no one there. She went back down again and into the kitchen.

"Did you call me Mary?"

"No Miss."

"Ah, it must be a mistake. I thought I heard you call my name."

"No Miss, it's probably the wind outside you can hear."

"Yes, I'm sure you're right," said Sheila as she exited the kitchen and began her climb up the stairs once more.

Back in her bedroom, Sheila quickly set up her computer and laptop and began typing away.

There it was again, a voice calling her name. Sheila went

over to the large bay window and looked out. Yes, the pine trees were blowing in the wind and she could see the moon through the giant Oak tree by the side of the drive. She shrugged her shoulders and went back to work.

Sheila was deeply engrossed in building her new website when a knock on her bedroom door made her jump.

"Come in Mary." She said.

The door opened about six inches.

"Come in. Have you brought my supper Mary?"

The door opened a little wider. Sheila got up from her computer and went over to the door. There was no-one there. Then she heard footsteps on the stairs and saw Mary coming up with a tray of food.

"Ah, Mary. Did you forget something?"

"Forget something? Not sure what you mean Miss."

"You came with my supper and opened the door and went away again."

"No Miss, I've only just got your supper done and brought it up this minute."

"Well, the door opened for some reason."

"Ah, probably the wind, as I said earlier."

"Yes, you must be right. I've looked outside and it is rather windy out there."

"Yes, Miss. That'll be what it is. The wind. Will that be all Miss?"

"Yes, thank you Mary. I'll see you in the morning and we can go over the rooms together. Good night Mary."

"Goodnight, Miss."

Sheila sat at the small table in the bay window and ate her supper. When her plate was empty, she drank the cup of tea and went back to her computer but was feeling rather drowsy and so decided to call it a day and get ready for bed.

As Sheila lay in bed, she thought she saw the curtains moving and as she could hear the wind whistling through the window frames, she thought nothing of it. She turned out the bedside lamp, rolled over onto her side and tried to sleep.

Creaking noises startled her, and she sat up. By now the full Moon had moved across the sky and was clearly visible through the bay window. Sheila watched the clouds floating by it and admired the stars, then lay her head back on her pillow.

More creaking noises filled the room and the wind howled louder through the gaps in the old windowpanes.

Sheila found it hard to sleep in this strange room. She kept thinking of her own small room back in her mother's house. The cosy duvet and her belongings piled high on the chest of drawers.

Suddenly the bedroom door burst open. Sheila sat bolt upright.

"Is that you Mary? I've finished my supper. You can take the tray away."

Sheila heard a rustling sound. It reminded her of those Henry VIII films where the ladies wore voluminous skirts that swished as they walked the long corridors of the castles. She slid out of the four-poster bed and went to peep around the open bedroom door.

Sheila thought she saw a shadow at the end of the long landing. A sudden flash of white light attracted her attention. There was a movement in the shadows near the large, oak cupboard at the end of the landing. Next there was a faint musty smell where a small staircase led to what used to be the servants' quarters. She hesitated for a moment, ran back and grabbed her dressing gown and was just putting one arm in the sleeve when she heard a scream that appeared to come from the small staircase. Softly she crept along the landing, holding her breath as she went. There was no-one there. Only the sound of the rain beating heavily upon her bedroom windows echoed around the huge landing.

"Who is it?" Sheila said as she looked up the narrow winding staircase. There was no reply. Then another swishing sound came from behind her and in the shadows at the far end of the landing near her bedroom door she thought she saw the shape of a woman in a long gown.

The shape floated slowly toward her. She held her breath once more as he eyes grew wide with excitement.

"Yes," she thought. "Ghosts, hundreds of them. That's what I want. Bring it on," she said aloud.

Suddenly there were flashes of lightening, the feeling of a strong wind blowing down the landing. Curtains that draped the antique paintings moved and the whole area became icy cold.

Sheila heard a loud smashing sound coming from the entrance hall below. She looked over the banister and saw a glass vase had fallen off the small table and smashed on the chequered marble floor.

"Wow," said Sheila, I have ghosts," and that was all that mattered.

4

I AM THE CHAMPION

*O*ctava put on his leather suit of armour and placed his sword in the scabbard on his hip. He stood straight, feet slightly apart, feeling strong before the match. Broad at the shoulders, a muscular body, standing six feet six inches tall.

His aides, after helping him with his suit of armour, were putting the final touches to it. Smoothing it down over his back and chest. Checking if the pads were protecting his shoulders correctly. Tightening the belt that pulled in an already slim waist.

The smell of greased leather was in the air and the armour squeaked as layer rubbed against layer. He looked not unlike an Armadillo about to go to war.

Octava strode up and down feeling strong, ensuring the armour fitted correctly. Testing it as he twisted and turned his subtle body. He wielded his sword flashing it in the brilliant sunshine.

"By the lowering of the sun victory will be mine." He said as he held his sword high above his head.

His aides stood back and bowed to the man they admired.

Shareen watched the three men from a distance. Sheltering from the burning sun under a spreading tree.

She stepped forward; the hot sand burned her feet, but she carried on until she came alongside Octava.

"My lord, my love, may I have a word with you?"

"Yes, but hurry, I am in the tournament shortly."

"My lord you know your opponent, Dradoon is in love with my sister, Rosca, even though they are both already spoken for."

"Yes, but what has this to do with me?"

"Well, my lord. I can make sure you win this tournament and become the greatest fighter ever."

"How?"

"I can ask my sister, Rosca to flaunt herself at the ringside and tease Dradoon so that his mind wanders during the challenge."

The two aides listened to what Shareen had to say and nodded their heads in agreement.

"Master," said the first aide, "You are not getting any younger. You have been ill a while. This is a good plan that Shareen has devised. We beg you to think about it and go with it. We know you can win this fight, but we want to make sure of your success above all the odds."

"I will think about it." Said Octava as he held his sword, examining the sharpness of the blade and aligning his eye with the length, admiring the straightness of it. "I will ponder over what you have told me and let you know. A little help is always good, but you all know I am not one for cheating."

"But, my lord, this is not cheating. Dradoon is already in love with Rosca and a little flirting and temptation never did anyone any harm."

"All right then, but make sure Rosca is given a good place to stand as the arena will be packed. Make sure Dradoon can see her. Now leave, as I must prepare for battle."

The aides and Shareen went about their business in the small settlement. Octava was left to ponder over the idea. He stood and faced the sun, closed his eyes and prayed to the gods and asked if this plan meant that he was a cheat. Suddenly black clouds appeared overhead and a strong breeze blew sand in his eyes. He splashed water on them to wash the sand out so that he could see more clearly. Then he realised this was a reply from the gods to tell him that he was not seeing things as he ought. He was taken in by his mistress Shareen and her deceitful plan. He had to put a stop to it. However, it was now time to make his way to the arena and he could not see Shareen or his aides anywhere.

As Octava marched to the stadium he passed by a slave attending a horse.

"Slave."

"Yes, my lord."

"How long have you been tending horses?"

"Since I could hardly walk, my lord."

"You look the kindly sort and you manage that horse well. I have a proposition to put to you."

"Yes, my lord, I am listening."

"As you know I am due to fight Dradoon in the arena. People say several seasons have passed since we last fought. I have been unwell since the last full moon and they fear I may not win."

"But you are strong my lord."

"Yes. I feel fit. However, there is a group who have set up some trickery. Rosca, who is in love with Dradoon and he with her, even though they are both spoken for already, will be taken to the ringside by her sister Shareen. Rosca will then tease

Dradoon from the ringside so that he is distracted, and I can then slay him. I know I can win this match fairly without any trickery. I ask that you come to the arena, find Rosca and take her away to my quarters so that she does no damage and so that I can win this match honestly. In exchange I will make you a free man on the understanding that you tend my horses and mine alone. Are you agreed?"

"Yes, my lord. Most definitely, my lord. I will be at the arena and take Rosca away to your quarters so that you can win as you rightly should.

"Thank you, slave. I must be off to the arena now as the tournament is about to begin.

Octava sped off with long determined strides and entered the arena. Dradoon was waiting for him. The two men met face to face and then paraded around the arena showing off their sparkling swords.

Rosca and Shareena had made their way into the crowd. Rosca was waving a blue silk scarf. "Dradoon, Dradoon."

Dradoon pretended to ignore her but he could hear her cries above that of the crowd and he glanced her way.

The two men stepped into the inner circle in the ring and on the command of the ring master they drew their swords.

Meanwhile the slave pushed his way into the crowd searching for Rosca. He found her and grabbed her around the waist with one arm and placed a hand over her mouth. Rosca managed to push his hand to one side and screamed, "Dradoon, Dradoon."

Dradoon heard Rosca's cry for help and turned to where her voice came from in the crowd.

Octava seized the moment and plunged his sword deep into Dradoon's heart.

As the slave dragged Rosca away screaming Dradoon fell to the ground. Blood poured through his leather armour and spread across the sand in the arena.

Octava held his sword up high and roared, "I am the champion. I, Octava win again."

5

BRIAN'S BIG DAY

"Hello Brian and Emily. Welcome to the show-Second Chances. Has everyone been kind to you in the green room?"

Brian and Emily nodded in unison

"That's great. Now I just want to introduce myself to you as your host for today's show. I'm Peter Hammond and I'll be asking all the questions today. I'm sure my staff have explained most of what it's about to you already and I'm sure you've also been watching the show.

It's a great show and very high up in the rankings for audience views. Now Brian if you would like to stand over there on my left. Emily you stand here on my right. You can see the score board behind me and I have a view of another board behind you. The audience will also be able to see the board at the back. I'll explain what we do now, and then when we are ready to go live, I will count us in-3-2-1 and we'll be live. I will then explain it all again and interview you both for a couple of minutes for the benefit of viewers and our audience. Is that all clear? Any questions?'

Emily and Brian nodded in unison once more.

"So, Brian you stay over there on my left and Emily you stand here on my right. I will go through the questions starting with Brian as he won the toss earlier in the green room, or so I was told. I am sure you are aware of the theme of the show and as it is called Second Chances we take your second answer as the correct answer. So, your first answer must always be a wrong answer. Is that clear?"

Brian and Emily nodded again.

"And we are off-3-2-1. Good evening ladies and gentlemen and welcome to our fabulous show, Second Chances. This is your friendly host Peter the greeter."

Chuckles scurried around the auditorium. Brian gave a smile and nod to Emily and Emily responded with a little wave of her hand.

"Let me introduce our first contestant Brian who is already on a winning streak as he won the toss. (more chuckles from the audience) Brian, tell us a little bit about yourself."

"My name is Brian. I'm a carpenter by trade. I come from Lancashire. My hobbies are going to the gym and bird watching."

"Nice to meet you Brian. Now our second contestant is the lovely Emily, here on my right. Can you tell our viewers and the audience a little bit about what you get up to and where you come from?"

Emily coughed. "My name is Emily. I come from Devon. I have two little girls who are probably watching this show right now. I also own a florist shop. My hobbies are horse riding and cycling."

"Well done Emily and Brian. Thank you for introducing

yourselves. Now, Brian, we have the first of your two questions here. Remember, the name of the show is, Second Chances. Brian, what is the capital of Scotland?"

With a huge grin on his face Brian says, "Edinburgh."

Laughter is heard from the audience.

"Ah, Brian. Do you remember the name of the show is Second Chances? You have two questions Brian. I will ask you once again. What is the capital of Scotland?"

"Edinburgh."

"Ah, Brian. This is your FIRST question and then you will have a SECOND CHANCE, with your second question."

"Oh, um, Dunfermline?"

"Well done Brian. And now for your second question. What is the capital of Scotland?"

"Edinburgh?"

"Correct Brian. You now have ten points and ten pounds."

Brian breathes a sigh of relief and smiles nervously as the audience applauds his efforts.

"Now Emily for your first two questions. What is the capital of Wales?"

"Newport."

"Correct. And for your second question. What is the capital of Wales?"

"Cardiff."

"Well done Emily. You also have ten points and ten pounds. Now, the questions will get harder. Brian what pudding is Yorkshire famous for?"

"Rice pudding." Grins Brian.

"And your second question. What famous pudding do they have in Yorkshire?"

"Yorkshire pudding." Answers Brian as he jumps up and down with glee.

"Well done Brian. Now Emily, what oil is Spain best noted for?"

"Fish oil?" Responds Emily tentatively.

"Correct. And now for your Second Chance question, what oil is Spain noted for Emily?"

"Olive oil." Emily replies as she smiles across at Brian.

"Well done everyone. And now we have a tie breaker, so you need to be on the tips of your toes. The bonus money for the tie breaker is five hundred pounds and that goes on top of your present amounts of forty pounds each. So, a great deal of money is at stake."

Brian stands on the tips of his toes to echoes of laughter around the auditorium.

"For your next two questions Emily and Brian you will need to shout out the answers. The first answer is the one I can take for each question. Are you ready?"

Emily and Brian nod to the affirmative.

"Question one. What is the name of the famous large expanse of water in Scotland that is noted for its monster?"

"Loch Ness." Shouts Brian as he bounces up and down.

"Ah, sorry Brian but that is the wrong answer."

"It's the right answer." Yells Brian as he points to the audience and then at Peter the greeter.

"No, sorry Brian it's the wrong answer to QUESTION ONE. And Emily has a one hundred pounds bonus because of your incorrect answer. Now let's get to the second tie breaker question."

"But I was right about Loch Ness and the monster Peter. This isn't fair." Said Brian as he stepped across the stage.

Peter turned to the camera crew and asked, "Can we cut this please?"

"No, sorry mate, we're live." Said Patrick, the chief cameraman.

"Come on Brian, let's play fair now. If you wouldn't mind going back and standing on that cross painted on the floor, then we can go onto the second bonus question. You still have a chance Brian."

Brian huffed and puffed and went back to stand on the special cross.

"For our final two questions on this lovely show, SECOND CHANCES, I will ask Emily the first question as Brian got this one wrong. Emily, what is the name of the large expanse of water in Scotland that is famous for its monster?"

"Lake Windermere."

"Absolutely correct Emily. And now for our final answer in this competition and for the bonus of five hundred pounds. What is the name of the large expanse of water in Scotland, noted for its monster?"

"I'm not doing this anymore." Shouted Brian. "It's ridiculous. You ask the same question twice. You don't give anyone a chance. I gave you the right answer and I'm due the five hundred pounds."

Brian marched toward Peter, his arms flailing. Murmurs erupted in the auditorium. Peter stepped back confused at what was now happening on his beloved stage. Peter turned to ask the chief cameraman to stop filming. Brian stepped closer and thrust his fist forward hitting Peter square on the nose. Peter fell over clutching his bloody face in his hands. Emily darted forward and stood between Brian and Peter, arms outstretched protecting him from another assault by Brian.

"Leave it Brian. Leave it. It's just a game show." Said Emily as she bent over Peter and offered him a tissue.

"To you it might be but to me it's worth six hundred pounds. I gave the right answer and this pillock refuses to give me the money. It's all a big con. Let me get my hands on him. Stand back."

Brian was about to throw another punch when the chief cameraman grabbed him by the throat, kneed him in the groin and left him doubled up on the floor.

"Right mate, you've had it now. You either get up and get out of this building and never ever come back again or I call the police. What's it going to be? There's no second chance."

Brian staggered to his feet, stuck one finger up at the audience, aimed a kick at Peter who was still lying on the floor, his head snuggled in Emily's lap and exited the stage left.

"Are you two okay?" The chief cameraman asked as he hovered over Emily and Peter.

"Yes, we're fine," said Emily as she stroked Peter's forehead.

"CUT," called the chief cameraman.

6

TRACY'S HALLOWEEN PARTY

"Hi Josie, are you nearly ready for Halloween tonight?"

"Yes, Tracy, just getting ready, really looking forward to it. If it's anything like last year then we will have a whale of a time. Can't wait."

"That's great Josie, me too. I've been busy all day cooking up some wonderful cakes and some brews. Would you mind phoning the others to make sure they know the time and my address, thanks. I'm rather busy just doing the finishing touches to the cakes and witchy goodies, so would appreciate it if you could call the other girls."

"No problem, Tracy, it's a pleasure. There should be about twenty of us if we all turn up. It will be a blast. Speak later, bye."

Tracy put her mobile down on the table and continued stirring up the cake mix. She did a mental check. Oven on, cake tins greased, food colouring in, then poured the green batter into the waiting paper cups and put the trays in the hot oven. Better check the clock too, she thought, as she made herself a cup of coffee.

Twenty minutes later the green cakes were ready to come out of the oven. She placed them alongside the orange ones she'd made earlier and the witches' brew punch she also made and the numerous bottles of home-made cider. She fussed about with the decorations of tinsel, paper ghosts, cobwebs and spiders that she'd scattered around the room and then sat down with a great sigh and drank her coffee.

Thirty minutes later there was a knock on the door.

"Do come in girls. Oh, you look amazing." Twenty young women burst into Tracy's hallway carrying bottles of booze, tins of cakes and biscuits and gifts galore.

"Put your bits and pieces in the kitchen and come and get yourselves a drink so that we can celebrate this wonderful Halloween night."

The girls rushed into the kitchen like a mob at a football match, grabbed a glass of cider each and a cheese nibble and sat in a circle in the lounge.

"Well, I am so pleased you have all managed to turn up this year." Said Tracy.

Giggles went around the circle of friendly witches.

"Karen, I do love your green hair. It matches the cakes I made." Said Tracy. More giggles went around the circle of friendly witches.

"And what about my orange hair to match my orange dress Tracy? I did it all myself. A bit of a mess but what the heck."

"You look fantastic, Sarah. You all look fantastic. Now come on girls, no time to waste, let's get these drinks down us and the food is all waiting in the kitchen."

The group meandered toward the kitchen pouring cider and punch into their glasses and downing it like there was no tomorrow, as they went.

"Whoops," said Megan, I feel a bit wobbly already."

"We've only just started," said Tracey. "Wait till later, when we get to dancing outside."

"Dancing outside. But it's freezing tonight." Said three of the girls in unison.

"Oh, you'll be all right once we get going. In any case I'm going to light a bonfire. Can someone help me, I should have got it lit by now."

"We will," said Sarah and Megan as Megan picked up a cigarette lighter by the back door and hurried outside.

Within a few minutes the bonfire was well alight and the girls began dancing around it, glasses in one hand and food in the other.

"This is amazing," said Josie. "I just so love bonfires and dancing around them." Josie began to cough as a sharp breeze blew some smoke from the bonfire in her direction.

Tracy smiled at her wonderful group of witchy friends, dancing, chatting, eating and drinking the night away.

"What's Megan up to?" shouted Tracy as she watched Megan slowly do a striptease. Megan carefully swapped her glass of cider between her hands as she wiggled out of her cardigan, dress, bras and knickers and stood there naked apart from her socks and trainers.

"Wow, you look a sight," Shouted Sarah above the crackling of the bonfire and the laughter of the other girls. "You could at least go the whole hog and take your shoes off as well."

"No," said Megan, I'm cold enough as it is, I'll have to run around the bonfire a bit more to keep warm. Megan ran around and around the bonfire like an Olympic athlete, spilling her cider as she went. Everyone stood back and laughed at her antics until their sides aches.

"Come on girls, have some more punch and cider," Said Tracy as she went around the group with the bottles. "Hey, is that

Brenda and Miranda taking their clothes off now?" Tracy laughed.

Soon all the twenty-one in the group were dancing naked around the bonfire. Cider and punch were flowing well, and the cakes were almost all consumed.

"Josie," called Tracy, help me get this top off the jacuzzi will you."

The two girls heaved the lid off the jacuzzi, and Tracy switched it on. "Come on girls, everybody in."

"But there's not enough room for us all," said Sarah.

"Yes, there is. Come on." Replied Tracy as she shuffled up again Josie.

Warm water splashed everywhere. The girls laughed and chatted and joked amongst themselves.

Suddenly a window in the neighbouring house flew open and a man leaned out. "Can't you lot shut the fuck up. Some people here are trying to get some sleep."

"Get stuffed," shouted Tracy followed by everyone's laughter.

"Woohoo," shouted Megan. "Come and join us your boring old fart."

"I'm going to call the police if you don't stop that racket and put the bloody bonfire out." Called the neighbour.

"Try it," shouted Megan and the girls all laughed once more.

"The police can come and join us." Said Sarah, and more laughter could be heard coming from the jacuzzi.

Five minutes later two policemen came in through the garden gate.

"Can I help you?" asked Tracy as she staggered , naked out of the jacuzzi with her cider glass still in her hand and tripped up a paving slab. The policeman caught her and tried to stand her upright.

"Thank you, officer." Said Tracy, that was very kind of you." She said between giggles. "Would you like a drink?"

"No thank you," said the officer, "I'm here because there have been complaints about the noise you are making."

"We're not making any noise, are we girls" Said Tracy as she turned to the group huddled in the jacuzzi.

"No," everyone said in a soft gentle voice.

"My friends are as good as gold officer." Said Tracy and she waved her arm at the jacuzzi full of innocent faces.

"Well we just had to check." Said the nice police officer as his mate stood and looked on with his mouth wide open.

"Come on Jack, shut that mouth of yours and let's get out of here." Said the officer as he pulled the young policeman by his arm. "Nothing much going on here at all."

"No sir," said the young policeman as he walked backward out of the gate, in the dark and tripped over the neighbour's cat that ran screeching across the lawn.

The girls all screamed with laughter.

Two minutes later the two policemen returned, completely naked, ran three times around the bonfire and then jumped into the jacuzzi on top of all the women.

Once more the neighbour opened his bedroom window and leaned out, but he saw very little of the policemen's bare bottoms through the thick smoke of the bonfire. He could still hear some giggling and lots of, "Oos" and "ahs" and he thought he heard someone say, "you naughty boy." Then he shut his window and went off to bed.

7

GOOD RIDDANCE

*T*he body lay face down on the floor, blood pooling from a large gash in the back of his head.

"What are we going to do with him Grandma? You didn't have to hit him that hard."

"I'm fed up with him pestering us for the rent when we cannot afford it. I lost my temper and my Golden Knitting Trophy from the Women's Guild, was handy, so I hit him over the head with it. Is he dead?"

"Yes, of course he is, you killed him outright. Now what on earth are we going to do with him?"

Maria turned to her husband Frank. "Come on Frank, you come up with some good ideas."

"Shall we put him in the freezer?"

"But he won't fit, the freezer is almost full."

"Well take out all the meat and peas and stuff and we can eat that during the week as it all thaws out. Then there will be room for the landlord to fit in there."

"I don't think so." Said Maria after looking inside and putting the freezer lid back down again. "We've got to act quickly. We need to get rid of his body and clear up all this blood. Valentina is bringing her new boyfriend for tea this evening. We cannot let them see this mess or the landlord looking like this."

"We'll just have to empty the freezer for the time being. Look, we can cook all the food as we're having a family meal tonight and that won't look so unusual. I'll start emptying the freezer right away. Grandma, you get some pots and pans ready and put the hot air fan in front of all the meat so that it begins to defrost." Said Frank as he hurriedly pulled out packets of carrots, runner beans and joints of meat from the freezer and lay them on the kitchen counter.

Grandma went into the cupboard and pulled out the electric heater, plugged it in and placed it on the counter in front of the meat. "Will that do Frank?"

"Yes, Grandma. Maria can you help me lift him? No, Grandma leave it to Maria and me, we don't want you hurting your back." Said Frank as he blocked Grandma from coming closer to the body and the freezer.

"Oh, my god," said Maria, he's so heavy.

Frank dragged the landlord by the arms and wedged him up against the freezer. Maria took his legs and pulled them around and then dropped them with a clank.

"Shall we take his shoes off?" Asked Grandma.

"What?' Said Frank.

"Shall we take his shoes off?"

"I don't know." Said Frank.

Grandma stood with her finger to her lips, thinking hard.

"I think it's probably best if we leave him as he is, otherwise, we'll have to do something with all his clothes and his bag." Said Grandma as she plonked his bag on top of his fat belly.

Maria said, "We don't have time to undress him and we'll

have to burn everything. We cannot have the neighbours complaining about us lighting a bonfire, now can we?"

"No," said Grandma.

"Come on Frank, let's get this over and done with. One, two, three, heave."

Maria managed to get the landlord's legs and feet over the side of the freezer. Frank gave one last push and the rest of the body fell in with a resounding thud, the head crashing up against a large chunk of ice and leaving bloody hairs dangling in the slight mist that was rising from the interior of the freezer. Grandma threw his bag in and slammed the lid down, almost catching Maria and Frank's fingers.

"Good riddance." Said Grandma as she went to put the kettle on. "Who wants a cup of coffee?"

"Coffee? Coffee? You can think of coffee at a time like this Grandma?" said Maria. "I've got to clear up all this blood you left."

"Oh, leave it and have a drink. It'll keep." Said Grandma as she continued to make three mugs of coffee.

"No, it won't keep, it'll dry and stain the floor and then we'll never get rid of the evidence. What on earth will Valentina and her new boyfriend think if they see blood everywhere?"

"Tell them we dropped a joint on the floor." Said Frank.

"No," Said Maria, "You two can just help me tidy this lot up. We need to put something on top of the freezer to keep the lid down and make things look normal again.

"I'll get a bunch of flowers from the garden, Maria and put that on top of the freezer. That will look pretty." Said Grandma as she trundled off into the garden with a pair of scissors and came back with a beautiful bunch of mini sunflowers. "They look really nice on top of the freezer, no one will know now."

"I hope not," said Maria as she kneeled down and scrubbed the blood stains off the floor."

Frank sat with his coffee and read the newspaper.

"Can't you help Frank?" Said Maria as sweat beads gathered on her forehead.

"I'm making sure the heater defrosts all this meat and veg' for you Maria. We don't want it all defrosting and dripping over the floor and making more mess for you to clear up."

*

"What time is it?" Asked Maria.

"Two thirty," said Frank.

"I'll have to start organising those joints then and get them ready for going in the oven." Maria took the baking trays from the shelves, placed the three joints of meat, beef, lamb and pork into the trays and left them to stand.

"Frank, you can put the veg' on when it's time."

Frank continued reading the newspaper.

"Grandma, you had better go and sit in your armchair and read a book and have a rest. You've had a very busy and traumatic day so far; we don't want any more mishaps."

Grandma took her coffee, picked up her book, turned on the t v set, sat down and immediately fell asleep and began snoring.

Maria looked at Frank who was otherwise engaged and tutted. She emptied the bloody water from the bucket into the sink and took the filthy cloth out to the dustbin, tutting as she went.

"Frank, can you put some tin foil around those three joints and get them in the oven please."

Frank did as he was told. "They won't all fit."

"Well they'll just have to. Shuffle them about. Just do something with them Frank. Valentina will be here in a couple of hours. We've just got to put on a good show and pretend that nothing has happened."

Frank shuffled the joints of meat about and then slammed the oven door shut. Grandma continued to snore, as Maria turned the volume down on the tv.

*

"What time is it Frank?" asked Maria

"Nearly four o'clock."

"Valentina will be here any minute now. Are the potatoes and veg' nearly done?"

"Yes, my darling. Do stop panicking. Everything is cooking nicely."

Maria looked out the bay window. "Here they are."

"Hello Mum," said Valentina as she gave her mother a hug. "Mum, Dad, Grandma, meet Cedro."

Cedro stepped forward and shook hands with everyone. "So, pleased to meet you all at last."

"Do sit down Cedro," said Maria pointing to the chair next to Grandma's. "Would you like a coffee? "

"I'll get us both one, Mum, you sit down for a minute."

"No, no!" said Maria and Frank in unison. Maria continued, "I'll make it. You and Cedro talk to Grandma and your father. I won't be a minute."

Cedro sat and spoke about his job and his 'prospects' in answer to the many questions fired at him by Frank and Grandma. Maria brought in the coffee, then went back into the kitchen to prepare the meal.

"Frank, can you come and help me serve dinner," said Maria. Frank told everyone to sit at the table and then went into the kitchen to help Maria. Frank pushed the lid to the freezer down hard and fiddled with the vase of flowers.

"Here you are everyone. I've got a lovely meal for us all."

Maria brought in a dish of roast potatoes and then went back for the two dishes of vegetables while Frank brought in the three joints of meat.

"That's a lot of food Mum, there's only the five of us."

"I know," giggled Maria, "but we Italians like to put on a good show for our visitors."

Valentina chuckled a little as she hung her head in embarrassment.

"Um... Mrs. Romano, I'm so sorry to trouble you but I'm allergic to carrots and beans and most other vegetables. I can only eat peas."

"Oh dear," said Maria.

"I'll go and get some peas from the freezer and put them in the microwave for you Cedro." Said Valentina.

"No!" said Frank and Maria in unison once more as Frank rushed to the kitchen door, almost blocking it with his body. Maria rose quickly from her chair and knocked It over. As she was straightening it up again, she said, "That's all right Valentina, your father and I can easily manage a few silly peas for Cedro, can't we Frank." Maria pushed Frank into the kitchen.

"Frank," Maria whispered, "pull the door up while I get some peas from the freezer, will you?"

Frank pulled up the door and stood guard. Maria covered her nose and mouth with her hand and rummaged underneath the landlord for a packet of peas.

"Here Frank, get these in a little water in the microwave as quickly as you can. I'll go and get another vase full of flowers and put that on top of the freezer along with the other one."

Maria took some scissors, hurried out into the garden and came back with a small bunch of sweet peas that she put in a vase next to the mini Sunflowers on the freezer lid. "That should do it." She said as she took the pot of peas out of the microwave and walked with them into the dining room.

"Here you are Cedro. Very fresh, straight from our freezer."

Grandma nearly choked on a roast potato. Frank sat down ashen faced.

"This meal is superb Mum, we'll help you wash all the dishes when we've finished. That's the least Cedro and I can do."

"No!" Frank and Maria spoke in unison once again.

"What is it with you two, Mum and Dad, you seem rather jumpy tonight? I know you've never met Cedro before, but I can assure you both the meal was lovely, and you are great parents."

"Oh, we're just a bit tired after a very hectic day, that's all dear." Said Maria.

Maria and Frank began to cough nervously. Frank nodded in agreement and pretended to yawn. Grandma put her hand to her face and made yawning sounds.

"Yes, it's been a really busy for all of us. A great deal of excitement and unexpected things happening." Said Grandma.

Frank looked across at Grandma and glared at her.

"Well you knew Cedro and I were coming around for tea and so that should not have been unexpected."

"No, your Grandma did not mean that, she meant um.. well I don't know what she meant." Said Maria.

"She meant we were not expecting Cedro to be such a nice young man." Said Frank.

Maria and Grandma nodded their heads profusely in agreement.

Maria yawned once more. "Well I really must say it was very nice having you both here Cedro and Valentina, but we are all very tired after a long, hard day." Maria said as she handed Cedro and Valentina their coats.

"Okay Mum, we can take a hint, but we'll be back at the weekend to see you all again."

"Oh! Oh, that will be... um... lovely, Valentina." Maria almost choked on her words as she walked to the front door and opened it.

"Bye, bye and have a safe drive."

"Bye," said Grandma

"Safe journey." Said Frank

*

Back in the kitchen Frank leaned up the freezer, his face drained of colour. "That was a bit close."

"Yes," said Maria," and they are coming back on Saturday."

"I know what we'll do." Said Frank.

"What?" asked Grandma and Maria at the same time.

"I'll order some ready mixed concrete and get that patio laid by the weekend.

"Good idea." Said Grandma, "I was about to suggest that myself."

Maria gave Grandma one of her looks. Frank got onto his computer to place the order for the concrete. Grandma tapped the freezer lid and said, "Good riddance, is what I say."

8

CHARING CROSS

"Bye honey, love you lots, take care."

"Bye Mum, we'll phone or text at each stage of our journey."

"Take care of her Harry."

"I will, Mrs. Bagshaw, um.. Mum." Harry chuckles. "It sounds so strange calling you Mum."

"You make such a lovely couple, now get on that train and get on with your honeymoon."

"Come on Anne, I'll help with the luggage." Harry heaves the two large rucksacks onto the train, stacks them in the luggage rack and searches for their seat.

"3A and 3B, here we are Anne. You sit by the window and wave to your Mum."

Anne raises her hand to her lips, blows kisses and mouths, 'love you,' as she wipes the tears from her eyes.

"I've never been on holiday without Mum before, it seems so strange," said Anne as the tiny figure of her mother disappeared from view.

Barbara's Shorts

"Well we are a couple now, my darling wife." Harry said as he gave Anne a hug.

"I know, it feels really weird to be married at last and on our honeymoon. How long is the journey?"

"Thirty minutes will get us into London and then we've got ten minutes max to get our connection. We won't need to rush but no dawdling either."

"I don't dawdle."

"I know you don't, just joking, that's all."

The catering trolly arrived and the newly married couple take coffee and sandwiches.

Harry looks at the time on his mobile phone. "Better make a move Anne. I'll help get your rucksack on your back and we can be first to exit."

Harry heaves the bulging rucksack onto Anne's back, and she loops the straps around her arms.

"We need the underground to the airport. I'll go first and you can follow as I've done this trip a few times with work."

The train comes to a steady halt and the young couple alight.

"Bloody hell Harry, that's a steep escalator, I'll get vertigo."

"No, you won't, just stay close behind me and look at your feet when you get on."

Suddenly a crowd of people came hurrying around the corner from the platform.

"Hang on a minute, let this lot pass, we don't want to get separated.

"Where are they all rushing too?"

"I don't know, maybe they're like us and need to get to their connection quickly."

"They don't look very happy."

"Come here Anne, stand against this wall and let them all go by."

57

More and more people came rushing past crowding the hallway and blocking the escalator. Anne and Harry pressed themselves tightly against the cold, tiled wall.

Suddenly there was a rush of hot air and people began to scream.

"Harry, what's happening?"

"I don't know. Stay still, stay with me."

An almighty blast sent Anne and Harry crashing into the wall near the bottom of the escalator. People were screaming, children crying, an elderly man collapsed on the ground and was trodden on.

Thick black smoke bellowed through the tunnels.

"Anne, where are you?"

"I'm here," said Anne as she grabbed Harry's rucksack.

"Keep low," shouted Harry, as he pushed Anne to the floor and began to choke on the fumes.

"We may have to ditch our rucksacks."

"No, please, no, it's got all my best stuff in it."

"Harry crouched beside Anne and ran his hand up her arm, it was difficult to see in the thick smoke. He pulled her scarf up around her mouth. "Keep your mouth covered."

People were staggering everywhere, and Harry had to push those away who fell onto him.

"Here Anne, look, wet your scarf with this water." Harry fumbled about in the dark, took the lid off his water bottle and wetted Anne's scarf and did the same for his own.

"We've got to get out of here Anne."

"How? I can hardly see a thing; the smoke is choking me."

"Come on, dump your rucksack and keep hold of my hand."

The newlyweds let go of their rucksacks and crept along the wall feeling as they went.

Harry found the bottom of the escalator, but it appeared to

have stopped moving and people were clambering over each other trying to climb up the stationary steps.

"Here, Anne, we can put our rock-climbing techniques into practice and get out of here. You'll have to feel your way along as best you can. I'll go first. I'm going to climb onto the centre of the escalator and hang onto the edges and pull myself up. You follow me. You do the same," Harry shouted above the raucous.

He dug his trainers into the steep, smooth sides of the escalator and gripped the edges firmly with his hands and slowly but surely eased himself up the centre piece of the escalator. Harry could sense Anne struggling behind him.

"Come on Anne, you can do it."

"I can hardly breathe Harry. You go on without me."

"No! Never, just keep going. We'll make it."

Harry struggled onwards up the steep escalator, people all around him screaming, shouting and climbing over each other in an effort to get out into some fresh air.

The smoke grew thicker and the heat intensified. He reached out for Anne but could not feel her behind him.

"Anne, Anne, he called between choking coughs."

Then he felt her hand on his ankle. A huge sigh of relief went through his body.

Harry continued up the steep climb, pressing his trainers into the sides of the escalator in order to get a grip and pulling himself up with his hands but the escalator began to feel hotter and hotter and the smoke thicker and thicker.

Then he saw a small flash of daylight and people wearing yellow high visibility vests. They were almost there.

Harry reached the end of the escalator, jumped down and stretched out his hand into the darkness for Anne. He could not feel her.

"Anne, Anne, where are you?"

He stretched his hand out again and felt a hand.

"I can't make it Harry; I'm exhausted and my chest hurts."

"Hang on in there Anne."

Harry grabbed the shoulders of Anne's coat and dragged her with all his might to the top of the escalator where she slumped in a heap on the ground among what seemed to be hundreds more writhing bodies.

Suddenly Harry could hear alarms ringing, police sirens, loudspeakers, people shouting instructions, but it was all a blur.

He grabbed Anne's coat once more and dragged her along the ground, keeping down himself to avoid the heavy, black smoke that continued to emerge from the tunnel. Then out into daylight.

Utter chaos greeted him. Ambulances, fire engines, police, bystanders.

Harry struggled onwards dragging Anne's limp body along the pavement until he could sense fresh air and fewer people. His eyes were watering, he could hardly breathe as he became nauseous and dizzy.

He felt a hand on his shoulder and looked up. There was a medic whose mouth was moving but Harry could no longer hear anything. The medic took hold of Harry's fists that were tightly clenched around Anne's coat, uncurled his fingers and helped him into the waiting ambulance while another man put an oxygen mask over Anne's face.

Suddenly Harry could hear again the noise was deafening, shouting, screaming, sirens a mass of tangled noises going through his numb brain.

"Anne, Anne." He pointed to his wife laying still on the pavement.

"She's going to be all right. What's her name?"

"Anne, her names Anne. We just got married today."

"And your name?"

"Harry."

"Well congratulations Harry, you're both going to be all right. The ambulance with take you to Charing Cross hospital. You're in safe hands now.

The paramedics lifted Anne up into the ambulance and placed her on a stretcher next to Harry. The young newly married couple lay alongside each other holding hands. Harry tried to lift his head and felt nauseous again. The paramedic gently re-adjusted the oxygen mask that had slipped to one side.

Harry squeezed Anne's hand and she squeezed his back.

Harry breathed a sigh of relief and passed out.

9

THE GHOST WHO COULDN'T FRIGHTEN PEOPLE

*J*an sat on her bed snuggled up with her duvet wrapped around her and her book, Dracula, opened at Chapter 1. She began to shiver, even though she felt warm. She took her cup of hot chocolate from the bedside table and began to sip it as she read.

She tried to convince herself that she wasn't in the least bit afraid even though the hairs on her arms were standing on end and she hadn't even got to the bottom of the first page!

Before she could continue reading, she thought she heard a creaking noise coming from the corner of the bedroom.

Don't be daft, she thought to herself and carried on reading.

She heard the noise again and then there was a rustling sound. She took the torch out from under her covers and shone it into the corners of the room that were not lit by her bedside lamp. There was nothing there. Back to her book.

Another noise made her look up and by the door stood what she thought was her younger brother Tim with a white sheet over his head and two slits for his eyes.

"Oh, do stop messing about Tim it's way past your bedtime and I'm trying to read."

There was no reply.

"Tim, go away, I said."

The white sheet appeared to stand more upright. Jan jumped out of bed, ran over to the sheet and went to grab it.

"Tim, I told you to stop messing about and get back to bed. You don't frighten me."

Jan reached out to pull the sheet away, but her hand went straight through it as if it were made of air. She did it again.

"Tim, is that you? What are you playing at? I'm going to call Mum if you don't stop this."

Jan tried to grab the sheet once more but again her hand went straight through thin air.

Then she heard sobbing coming from under the sheet and the sheet seemed to crumple into a heap on the floor.

"What on earth is going on? Who are you? You don't frighten me."

"That's the whole point," A faint voice said between sniffles, "I don't frighten anyone."

Jan put her hand over her mouth to try and stem the laughter that was erupting from deep in her stomach.

A ghost that can't scare anyone. She thought. Well he ought to read the Dracula book to get some ideas.

"Well I don't know what you can do about that Mr. Ghost, or how I can help you. I've just tried to touch you and my hand went straight through the sheet. Anyway, wearing a silly old white sheet with two holes in for your eyes isn't going to scare anyone."

"But I don't know what else to do," sniffled the white sheet, "I've tried loads of things, like being a dragon."

Suddenly the white sheet became an orange dragon about the size of a Labrador dog and fire was shooting from its nostrils.

"Wow," said Jan, "But stop all that fire or you'll set my room alight."

"It's not real fire," said the dragon. "and that's why people aren't scared of me."

"You're not a very big dragon either, are you?" Said Jan.

"No, said the dragon," as he began to cry large, golden dragon tears that pooled in a puddle on the bedroom floor.

"Look, you've now made the floor all wet with your tears. Can you stop it dragon and I'll try and help you become a bit scarier?"

"You haven't got any wings, have you? Dragons have wings."

"Do they?"

"Yes."

"Like this?" the dragon appeared to sprout two tiny wings on either side of its body.

"But they're no good, Dragon, they'll get you nowhere, they're tiny."

"But I can only grow big wings when I'm a dragonfly or a butterfly."

"Look, let me pull on your wings and see if I can make them any bigger."

Jan stepped forward, reached out her hand but once again it went straight through the dragon.

"You'll have to make yourself, more real, more solid somehow. My hand keeps going straight through you."

"I'll try," sobbed the dragon as more golden tears fell to the floor.

The dragon huffed and puffed some huge flames and then stood up taller.

"Like this? Touch me now and see what happens."

"That right," said Jan as she touched the dragon.

"Oh, you feel very soft. Here let me pull on your wings and see if that makes any difference to their size."

"Ouch," said the dragon," that hurt."

"Sorry, I didn't mean it. Let's try something different. What you need is a castle, like Dracula has."

"Whose Dracula."

"He's the man in the book I'm reading. He's a Count, Count Dracula and he lives in a huge castle and drinks blood."

"Oh, I hate blood, I'm a vegetarian. My favourite food is cabbage. Any leftovers that little children leave on their plate, then I eat it all up."

"Oh, well you'll love my brother Tim as he hates cabbage and he hides it under his plate and tells Mum he's eaten it all."

"I know," said Dragon, that's how I came to be here, I've been eating his cabbage for years."

Jan began to laugh so much that it hurt her stomach and she had to hold her sides to stop them hurting as well.

"What's so funny about that?"

"A dragon who goes around in a white sheet and cannot grow proper wings and cannot scare anyone and eats only cabbage. That's what's funny."

Jan began laughing again and had to sit on the floor but accidently sat in the puddle of golden tears.

"These tears are warm." Jan ran her hands through the golden tears.

"Hurrah you can touch the tears and you can touch me now."

Jan gave the dragon a hug and kissed his nose.

"Come on, let's talk about this castle that you need."

Suddenly a small fort appeared in the centre of Jan's bedroom.

"No, that's not a castle, that's a fort and it looks just like the sort Tim would play with. You'll have to do much better than that. Look, let's go out into the garden where you will have more room and you can build a giant castle there."

Instantly the dragon disappeared.

Jan looked out of her bedroom window and saw him sitting under a pine tree by the lawn.

Well, I wish I could do that, I've got to put my slippers on and run down two flights of stairs before I get to be outside. Jan put her feet into her slippers and as she walked to her bedroom door she went through the golden puddle of tears, the next minute she was on the lawn beside Dragon.

"Wow. Your tears must be made of magic. I trod in the golden puddle and now here I am. I can fly. I can fly."

Jan spread out her arms and suddenly shot away around the top of the pine tree and back down again.

Dragon laughed. He had never seen a human flying unaided before. He was beginning to feel braver now but not scarier.

"That's lovely, I'm so glad you can fly but I still want to be scary. I want to frighten people to bits."

Jan laughed at Dragon's endearing desire to frighten people.

"Look, I'll show you some tricks. My brother Tim is always trying to frighten me. Go and hide behind that tree."

"What for?" Said Dragon.

"Because I want to show you how to frighten people."

The dragon trundled off behind the tree and was just about to fall asleep when Jan crept up on him.

"Boo!"

The dragon's eyes shot open and he jumped two feet in the air.

"Don't do that Jan you frightened the life out of me."

"There you are then Dragon, that's what you've got to do. Come on, I'll hide, and you creep up on me and try to make me jump."

Jan hid behind the tree. Dragon stomped along swishing his tail.

"No, dragon you're making far too much noise. You must creep up on me."

"Oh, all right then if you say so."

Dragon tried again. He trod carefully and stood by the tree.

"Boohoo."

"No Dragon, that will not do at all. You must shout, BOO as loud as you can and even stamp your feet and clap your paws. You must try harder if you want to be a scary dragon."

"I'll try just this once and then I'm going to give up."

Dragon crept up to the tree, took an almighty in breath and bellowed, "BOOOOOO," so loudly that it shook the pine tree and rattled all the glass windows of the house and nearly shattered them all.

Jan jumped so high that she hit her head on an overhanging branch.

"Ouch Dragon, not only did you nearly burst my ear drums, but you made me bang my head."

"Sorry." Dragon bowed his head.

"No, that's all right, all is forgiven now. You've done it, you've learned how to be scary. We must now make your castle because scary dragons must have a castle to live in."

In an instant There was a giant fortress of a castle in the front garden of the house.

"That looks magnificent Dragon. Now you're learning."

Dragon jumped up and down and wagged his giant tail with joy.

"I'm beginning to get it now, thank you Jan. I think I can be a scary dragon after all.

"Tell you what Dragon."

"What."

"You stay here, and I'll go and get my little brother Timothy and you can practice on him. If you can scare Tim, then you can scare anyone."

Dragon rubbed his front paws together with glee.

Jan ran off into the house and tapped on Tim's bedroom door.

"Are you awake Tim? I've got something I want to show you."

"What, is it Jan, you woke me up."

"Sorry but it's rather important. Can you put your dressing gown and slippers on and come with me into the garden? There's something magical I want you to see."

"Magical?"

"Yes, magical."

Tim put on his dressing gown and slippers and followed Jan down the hall to the front door.

"Look," said Jan.

"Wow, it's a castle. Where on earth did you get that from Jan?"

"Well, my friend built it."

"They built it quickly then didn't they." Said Tim as he moved nearer the castle, his mouth wide open in awe.

"I want you to walk around the outside of the castle and have a look and tell me what you think.

Tim yawned as Jan pushed him to her right. When Tim had turned the first corner and was out of sight Jan beckoned Dragon to come close.

"Dragon, you go to my left and creep around the castle and then when you're near Tim make him jump, like I showed you."

Jan pushed Dragon to her left and waited.

After what seemed like ages Jan heard an almighty roar coming from the back of the castle walls. She saw flames rising high above the roof and treetops. Then Tim shot past her at break-neck speed, the blood drained from his face, and hid in the bushes by the front door.

"Jan, Jan," Tim whispered, "Get here quick, there's a dragon in the garden."

Jan lay down on the grass and rolled about laughing.

"You've done it Dragon, you scared my little brother Tim. Nothing has ever scared him before. No spiders, frogs or snakes-nothing. Congratulations Dragon."

"You mean you can talk to the dragon, Jan."

"Yes, he's my best friend and I've been teaching him how to scare people as he could not scare me when we first met. He also built this castle."

"Wow, Sis, that's amazing. He really did frighten me but if you say he's your friend then can he be my friend too?"

"Yes, of course he can. Dragon. Dragon, come on over and meet my little brother Tim."

Tim stepped backwards with fright, but Dragon held out his paw and gently took Tim's hand and shook it.

"Friends?"

"Yes, friends," said Tim and the three friends hugged and then sat on the grass and laughed until their sides ached.

"Well, you two, I've got to go now. Thank you for showing me how to frighten people, I shall forever be grateful to you. I'll come back and visit you both and tell you how many people I've frightened and how I did it. Bye."

With a puff of smoke Dragon and the castle disappeared.

"Come on little Tim, we'd better get back to bed before Mum finds us out here on the lawn in our nightclothes."

"Okay Sis, I'm very tired. One thing though. I wasn't really scared of that dragon. I just pretended to be."

"Yes, I know," giggled Jan. He didn't frighten me either.

10

JAMES' FIRST YEAR

James hated having to wear a red sash to indicate he was a newbie at St. Thomas' Boarding School for boys. He felt as if he had been singled out by some kind of spotlight above his head. Like a police helicopter shining its beam on an escaped criminal. As it was, he felt trapped, nowhere to go, no one to run to when he felt down. He walked the long corridors staring at the floor, not wanting to annoy any of the other boys. He'd seen how the long termers treated the newbies. Taunting, teasing, bullying.

"Hey fatto, want some chocolate?"

He felt sorry for Edward who was considerably overweight and everyone, even the new boys seemed to pick on him.

"Hey, skinny, we'll miss you if you turn sideways."

James had always been on the thin side.

Two weeks after joining the school Edward and James were walking back through the grounds after a rather bad game of rugby where Edward found it hard to run and James got knocked over by every tackle.

"Hey, fatty and skinny. You make a great twosome." The voices came from a group of six lads who were standing beneath a tree and sharing a cigarette.

"Did you hear us? Hey, stop, we want to talk to you."

Edward and James began to walk faster. They would soon be at the entrance to their rooms.

The group began to run toward the two boys.

"We said stop." The tallest lad ran and stood in front of Edward and James. They had no alternative but to stand still.

"Like rugby, then do you?" The lad continued. Another boy grabbed James' boots and threw them across the lawn.

"Leave my friend's boots alone." Said Edward.

"And?" Said one of the other boys.

"Nothing. Just leave us alone."

"Come on boys, let's teach them how to do a tackle."

Two of the group grabbed Edward's arms while another got him with a headlock.

James kicked the boys in the shins but to no avail. Another lad grabbed James around the waist and pulled him to the ground.

Meanwhile Edward had managed to squirm himself free from the headlock by putting all his weight into swinging himself around. He then brought his Rugby boot down onto the head of the boy who was rolling on top of James.

Another boy ran over and Edward bashed him in the face with his other boot. Then he kicked the shins of two more boys.

"Leave my friend alone will you or you'll know who you're messing with."

The gang gathered together, fists raised but then the evening bell began to chime, and the group of lads ran off hugging their wounds.

"Are you all right James?"

"Yes, just a bit bruised that's all. You can put up a good fight when you want to."

"Yes, I guess it helps when you carry extra weight."

"Thanks, thanks a lot but we'd better mind they don't all gang up on us again later on. I'll keep an eye out for you and you can do the same for me."

"Yes, we need to stick together." The two lads did a high five.

*

The following day it was the inter class swimming contests.

Edward and James stood at the end of the pool waiting for their races.

"Look at fatty and skinny," Said one of the boys who had attacked them the day before. "You don't stand a chance. Think you can swim mate and beat me? You've got another think coming, I've been the champ here since day one." Said Kaden.

Edward walked over to the blocks and stood at lane 6 while James stood near the blocks for lane 5. Giggles could be heard all around.

"Now, now lads, silence or we won't hear the gun go off." Said the swim coach.

"Take your marks." The swim coach lifted the starting pistol up in the air and fired.

James was the first off the blocks and into the water, swimming with long, deliberate strokes. He skimmed through the water like a slithery fish.

Edward threw his arms back and then forwards and dived in like a torpedo shot from a submarine. He stayed under water for almost a quarter of the length of the pool and was just behind James.

"Old fatty will soon run out of puff." Shouted a boy who was waiting for the next race.

"Come on Kaden, show 'em what you've got. You can't let them beat you champ." Shouted a large group.

James was the first to tumble turn at the far end followed by Edward who did another quarter length underwater which brought him alongside James. They swam neck and neck for the next length then for a few metres Edward overtook James. By this time Kaden was flagging considerably and was now in fourth place.

"Kaden, Kaden." Shouted the group on the poolside.

"Someone stop that fat idiot and old skinny bones." Came a loud voice from the group.

Edward and James swam on. The last turn, it was neck and neck. Down the final length Edward was in front and at the very last second James stretched out his fingertips as far as he could and touched the wall followed by Edward. The two boys looked at each other, pumped their fists in the air and hugged each other over the lane ropes.

The third lad glided in rather badly followed by the now ex-champion Kaden who immediately got out of the water and was disqualified.

A huge roar from all the newbies went up and they chanted, "James, Edward, James, Edward."

At the trophy giving James stood on the rostrum in first place, Edward in second place, they shook hands and received their medals.

Kaden, the gang leader was nowhere to be seen.

Edward and James went into the changing room and as they entered a boy slammed the door shut. The gang, minus Kaden had arrived.

"Just try it," said Edward as he held his fists in the air and stepped toward the leading lad.

"No, that's all right, calm down. We just came to congratulate you both, that's all."

Edward hesitated.

"Okay, but you'd better come in peace."

"Yes, we want to be friends now. You two are the new champions. Never thought you'd be able to swim like that. Not with you being ….."

"Fat," said Edward as he laughed.

"No, I didn't mean that at all. You just don't look like a swimmer that's all, and James looks a bit feeble, maybe. Took us all by surprise."

The group turned and scrambled back through the door of the changing room.

Edward and James looked at each other and did a high five.

"Pals?"

"Pals it is."

"Thanks for being there for me Edward," said James.

"No problem. What are mates for if we can't look after each other."

"Too true." Said James as he threw his red sash in the bin. It was the end of his first year at the boarding school and as a newbie.

11

EM AND THE BLUE FAIRY

*E*m picked up her mobile and sighed.

"Emily, have you still got your light on. It's time to drink your milk and get to sleep. I don't want to have to come all the way up there now do I?"

"No Mama and yes Mama, I've had my milk and turned out the light." She picked up the glass of milk and immediately put it back down again.

"Goodnight then and I'll see you in the morning for breakfast."

"Goodnight Mama."

Em put her mobile on the bedside cabinet, switched on her torch and continued reading.

Em loved to read about fairies but her latest book was no ordinary fairy book. It was also a pop-up book. In the centre when she spread the pages a beautiful blue fairy stood up. Her wings glistening with gold and silver sparkles.

Em spent most of her time admiring the fairy and less time actually reading the story.

"I do wish I could speak with you and play with you." Said Em.

"You can."

"What?"

The fairy jumped from the page, flew around Em's head and landed on her nose. Em went boss-eyed.

"But you're real."

"Of course, I am. You made a wish and it was granted. I'm here to speak and play with you."

"How wonderful and magical, I never knew that."

"Ah, but you never wished before."

"I've often wished for a playmate, but Mama says there aren't any children within miles of The Old Manor House and besides she says she doesn't want little kids messing up her shiny wooden floors. So, she puts me here in this bedroom right at the end of the long corridor. I'm so far away from everyone else that we have to communicate by our mobiles. She says it's so the noises around the house don't keep me awake at night, but there's no-one here to make any noise. There's just Mama, my tutor and the two ladies who work in the kitchen. The only noises I hear are the stairs and the wooden panelling creaking all night long and that keeps me awake and frightens me sometimes.

"Those noises you hear Emily."

"Em, it's Em."

"Those noises you hear Em are not the stairs and wooden panels creaking but all the little creatures from all your books. They all come alive at night, but you are fast asleep and don't know this."

"Really?"

"Yes, Really."

"But I never see anyone. I generally have the milk my tutor gives me and then fall asleep soon afterwards."

"I think your tutor puts a little sleeping draft in your milk each night so that you don't bother her and so that she can watch t v till the early hours. I'll tell you what."

"What?"

"Tonight, don't drink any milk. Look, why don't you open the window and pour it out there and just pretend that you drank it."

Em pulled hard on the metal clasp, opened the window and poured the milk into the thick Ivy leaves that clung to the outside of the building.

"Now, I will sit with you and we'll wait and see who wakes up first."

Em sat on her pillow, drew her knees up and wrapped her arms around them. She scanned the room with her torch.

"No, turn your torch off and wait until you hear some noises. Then you can shine a light on whatever it is."

Em switched the torch off and cupped her hands around the backs of her ears in order to hear better.

After what seemed ages, she heard a rustling sound. She pointed the torch beam toward where she thought the sound was coming from and saw a huge Tiger. She screamed and threw herself underneath her duvet.

"It's all right Em, you can come out, he's friendly."

"But he's huge with bright orange eyes and white fangs."

"But he's only come alive from your book and so he's quite harmless."

The Tiger crept over to Em purring softly as it rubbed its face along the side of Em's four poster bed. Em stretched out a shaking hand and stroked it's head. The Tiger placed a paw, twice the size of both Ems hands put together, on the bed.

"Nice Tiger, nice boy." Em said even though her voice was shaking.

Suddenly there was a scraping noise coming from outside Em's bedroom door.

"What's that noise Blue Fairy? Can I call you Blue Fairy?"

"Yes, of course. Shall we go and investigate?"

The fairy flew to the door and Em had to run to catch her up. Em pulled on the giant brass knob and heaved the solid oak door open. She was about to let out another scream when the fairy slid inside her mouth and almost choked her.

Em spat the fairy out.

"What on earth did you do that for fairy?"

"We don't want you screaming and waking everyone up now do we?"

"But there's a huge Bear ov…over th…there," Said Em as she pointed to a giant Brown Bear who was sitting on one of her mother's best chaise longues. Mama will kill me if he leaves a single hair behind or if he scratches anything. She"ll blame me, I'm sure of it. Em began to cry.

"Look Em, all is well. These animals, and maybe more creatures, only come out of your books at night. They mean no harm. Have you ever seen any evidence of the Tiger or the Bear in your bedroom or anywhere else in The Old Manor House, or its grounds, for that matter?"

Em put her finger to her lips as she thought. "Well no, Blue Fairy, no I haven't and that's very strange. I've got so many books on my shelves about fairies, gnomes, dragons and unicorns and loads more about tame and wild animals. I've got one about a giant whale, but I've never seen any come to life like the Bear and like yourself Blue Fairy. What if we brought the giant whale to life Blue Fairy? That would be fun, wouldn't it?"

And with that there was a huge splosh sound that seemed to echo throughout the whole building. Em looked over the bannister to the giant hallway below. A massive whale had filled the entire area and was flapping its tail up and down.

"Oh, my goodness Fairy, he'll knock mum's silver all over the place with that tail."

"No, no, he'll be gentle with all your mother's fineries."

Just as Em and Blue Fairy were climbing onto the bannister for a better view of the Whale the tutor came out of her study carrying a glass of red wine and walked diagonally across the black and white tiled floor to the corridor that led to the kitchens.

"I don't believe this." Said Em, "my tutor has just walked straight through the Whale. I saw it with my own eyes. I must be dreaming."

"No, you're not dreaming Em. These creatures are from another realm, another dimension and so your tutor does not know they exist. She cannot see them. Only we can see them."

"Wow," said Em. "From another realm, another dimension."

"Come on Em, I'm going to cover you in magic dust, and we can invite the Tiger and Brown Bear to come and play with us and the Whale in your magnificent hallway, and I promise we won't damage any silver or that beautiful chandelier." Blue Fairy took out a miniature jar of blue dust and sprinkled it onto Em's head. Em was about to sneeze but Blue Fairy covered her nostrils with her glittering wings.

"We can't have your tutor, or anyone hear you sneezing, now can we?"

"No," giggled Em.

"Come on, let's hurry down the spiral staircase and go play with Whale, Tiger and Bear."

Em ran after Blue Fairy, followed by the two wild animals.

"I'm going to climb on Whale's tail and slide down his back." Said Em.

Whale put his tail down flat for Em to climb onto and then

gently lifted it up so that Em could sit on his back. Then Em slid down to the ground.

"Wheee. I want to do it again. "I've never had so much fun for ages."

Bear joined in and Em and Bear spent a full ten minutes climbing onto Whale's tail and then sliding down his sides.

"Oh, I'm all puffed out now Blue Fairy."

"Would you like to ride on my back?" Asked the Tiger.

Em nearly fainted and rushed over to sit next to Blue Fairy.

"That Tiger spoke to me. Am I going mad Blue Fairy?"

"No, of course not. You can play with these creatures and communicate with them, just as you are speaking with me. Would you like to ride on the Tiger's back?"

"I'd love to." Em yawned.

"I think Tiger should take you back to bed now as you appear to be getting tired. Maybe too much excitement for one day. We will all escort you to your room."

"But Whale is so big he won't fit in my room."

"Ah, but here is where the magic lies. Whale can make himself as big or as small as is necessary."

"Em stood on Tiger's front paw and lifted her leg over his back and hung onto his soft fur."

The group slowly went up the winding staircase, along the dark corridor to the back of the house and into Em's bedroom. Em's head began to nod and her eyelids felt very heavy.

Tiger stood beside her four-poster bed and Em rolled off his back. Bear and Blue Fairy pulled up her duvet. Blue Fairy switched off her torch and mobile phone and Whale fanned Em with a warming breeze with his giant tail.

Em was soon fast asleep.

"Come on fellas, we must get back inside Em's books. I'm

sure she'll call upon us all again tomorrow night now that she knows about the magic within herself and her books."

"Night, night, Em." Said Bear.

"Night, night, Em" said Tiger.

"Night, night Em." Said the giant Whale.

Blue Fairy landed on Em's pillow, sprinkled some more fairy dust, for good measure, blew her a kiss and with a flutter of her blue sparkling wings she vanished back inside Em's book.

12

FLYING SOUTH

Sarah looks perky this morning. She's sitting on that high branch over there singing her dawn song. I bet she feels the same as I do that it's about time we flew south. The wind is getting up, the temperature has dropped considerably. We cannot stay here much longer, or we will freeze or starve to death. Each day has shown fewer insects to eat. Each day there are less of the gang around. Ah, she's fluttering her wings I'd better stretch mine too.

And we're off, flying high up into the clear blue sky and catching the South Wind. Oh, it feels lovely to be able to spread my wings to their maximum and just glide for miles in-between flutters. Sarah is going well, and she appears to be ahead of me. I can also see a small group behind me. I must concentrate and press on. I'll keep one eye on my friends and the other on the sun and I'm sure we'll soon safely arrive at our summer quarters.

I can see the mountains of Scotland below me. There seems to be more snow about than usual I hope my pals there soon begin their journey south before it's too late.

I think I need to get a bit of altitude here. It's much easier to fly at a higher altitude. Sarah is way ahead of me now and soon she'll be out of sight completely. I can hear the geese and swans behind me. It seems everyone is catching me up and even overtaking me. I cannot flap my wings any faster, I was hoping to be able to do some gliding and not put out so much effort right at the beginning of my journey.

I think I need a drink and to find some food. Ah, I've just spotted a lake below I'm going to go for it and see if I can find food and take a little drink and rest.

Phew that was a bit scary and bumpy with the strong wind buffeting me all the time. I wonder if there are any insects hiding amongst these bushes and this Heather? That was a lovely meal. I feel quite full up now and so replenished. I'm going to get to the water's edge and have a drink and then set off South again.

What's that around my ankle? I can't move my leg. There's something wrapped tight around my leg and it hurts each time I flutter my wings and try to escape. Now it's wrapped itself around both my feet. I'm trapped. I can't move. I'm going to play dead and hope nothing comes to eat me up.

"Hey little fella, what's happened here. You got yourself all tangled up in fish wire."

I can hear a strange sound, and something has taken hold of me. I can't move. Whatever it is does feel quite warm but it's scary all the same. Something has grabbed one of my legs but now my leg feels much better and free. My other leg feels free as well. I can move my feet but this warm thing around me is stopping me moving my wings.

"There you are little chap, you're free from the fish wire now. Off you go."

Ooops, something has thrown me up in the air but my wings seem to be working perfectly and I'm soaring up high once again. I can see the geese and swans in front of me now. I need to get to a higher altitude where it is easier to fly and glide once more. Goodness knows what happened back there at the lake. At least I have a full belly, but I did not get a chance to drink any water. I will have to manage without it. The fluids from the little bugs I ate will have to suffice for the time being. I have a huge ocean to cross as well and no chance of fresh, clean water there.

Ah, I spy a small stretch of water. I will fly down and get a drink before I take the enormous trip across the ocean.

Agh, I feel trapped. I'm all tangled up again. Help, I can see a man coming towards me. I hope he doesn't hurt me.

"Come on little chap we've got to ring you. It won't take long."

Help, I'm now in some kind of dark bag and its swaying from side to side and making me feel sick. Oh, I'm being put on something hard now I can feel it through the bag. Someone is saying I'm a good weight. Well if I could find more food and water to eat and drink then I could keep my weight up. I must keep it up for the long flight over the ocean. I wish humans would leave me alone and let me fly to my destination in the hot country.

Agh, now they've got hold of my leg and are putting something on it. My leg feels a tiny bit heavier than the other one. I do hope It does not cause me to fly wonkily or I'll never get to my destination.

"All done and now you can continue on your journey little chap. We'll be keeping an eye on you though with our radar equipment."

Well I'm not sure I like the idea of being spied upon or this thing around my leg but there's very little I can do about it now. I must press on.

The sun is rising high nicely and there seems to be a great

deal of lift in the air and so I am off once more for my journey across the vast ocean.

There seem to be more ships about this time than my last sea crossing. More rubbish in the waters as well.

The sky is getting dark now, but I know I'll be okay. I can look up at the stars and if it does not rain I will fine.

At last I've reached the coast and it looks like some lovely green trees and grass and water below so I'll go and have a look and a rest and see if I can get something to eat and drink.

Ouch, I'm caught in a net again. This one seems different from the other one when the man put a ring on my leg. This net is filthy and coarse and is hurting me.

There's someone coming toward me.

"Please don't hurt me. Please don't hurt me."

It's a young boy. I can hear my friends all squealing and I don't know what is happening to them or what is going to happen to me.

I can hear someone calling out to the boy to get a move on.

"Yes dad, I'm just looking for birds at this end of the net, but I cannot see any."

What's he talking about. I'm here and I can see about five of my friends also trapped.

What's happening. The boy is unravelling their legs and wings from the net and setting them free.

"Hey pretty little thing, you are so tiny and colourful and I know you have flown a long, long way and are on your way to your summer nesting grounds. I don't want to eat you and I don't want my father and his brothers to eat you either. Here, let me loosen the strands from your legs and wings."

I decide to keep very still and quiet and hope that this little boy is telling the truth and that is that he does not want to eat me and won't give me to his father and brothers to be eaten. Oh, I feel so sorry for my friends they are going to go into the cooking pot or be caged and sent to another country in exchange for lots of money. My poor friends.

"There you are little one, you are now free. Fly free my friend and don't come back this way or you will get hurt."

Once again, I'm being thrown up into the air, but I gain my balance quickly and flap my wings as fast as I can in order to get out of this horrible place. I am very grateful to the kind little boy, but I do fear for my friends.

It is dawn and I am near my destination. I can sense it, smell it, see it, feel it. I am almost there.

Ah, look, the tall grass, the short, round bushes full of berries, the river with the mud filled with insects for me to eat. At last I am at my summer home.

I'm going to land by the water and have a long-awaited drink and eat some mud bugs.

Ah, I can see Sarah, I'm so glad she made it.

"Sarah, Sarah, I'm so glad you made it. Where are Frank and Billy?"

"They did not make it. Many of our friends got caught in the nets. Some were poisoned on the way, some lost their way, some got caught in that storm. What's that you've got around your leg?"

"It's a ring. I heard the man say it was so that they could keep a track on me, but I don't like it. I don't like it one bit."

"Is it heavy? Does it stop you from flying?"

"No, it's okay but just a bit cumbersome. I guess, after a while I won't even know it's there. I got caught in a net, but a kind boy set me free."

"Ah that's probably where many of our friends got caught and why they did not make it." Said Sarah.

"We need to think of another way to travel each year, but I

think a different route will put many more miles onto our journey and we may get lost on the way."

"Yes, and there will be prevailing winds that may drive us off our route as well. Best to keep to the same tracks each year and hope for the best." Said Sarah as she preened her feathers.

"Yes, I think that is what is needed, stick to the same routine and hope and pray all will be well each year. We've survived so far haven't we. And now it's time for me to put my head under my wing and rest. Good night."

13

BOOGIE WOOGIE BUGLE BOY OF COMPANY B

"Where am I?" She said as she tries to lift her head.

"You're in hospital my dear."

"But how did I get here?"

"A wall collapsed during the bombing last night. You were brought here, along with six others in the horse drawn ambulance."

"My head hurts and I can't feel my legs."

"You've had a bad blow to the head and I'm afraid your legs have suffered some damage. Here, take your medication and I'll get the doctor to come and visit you as soon as he can."

The nurse helps her lift her head as she sips her medication.

She glances across at the bandaged patient, propped up with three pillows and reading a newspaper. The front page displays the headline, ALL NIGHT HELL FOR NEW YEAR'S EVE 1917.

She falls asleep.

*

She carefully places the needle on the seventy-eight record, swaying to the music of Boogie Woogie Bugle Boy of Company B.

She splashes her face with warm water, pats it dry then sits at her dressing table and looks in the mirror. A hair band keeps her hair from her face as she reaches for her compact of peach foundation. Softly she places the tip of her middle finger into the cream then gives three dabs, one on each cheek and one on her forehead. Her face goes into contortions as she smooths the foundation with her fingertips and completely covers her face.

She takes a giant powder puff and pats powder on her nose, cheeks and forehead, leaving a cloud of pink dust around her head. She brushes the excess powder away. She examines her face for blemishes or missed places. An extra dab here, an extra blob there.

She takes her bright red lipstick and draws the outline of her lips. She spreads her mouth wide and covers her bare lips with red gloss.

She inspects her reflection in the mirror from every angle, pulls off the hair band and begins brushing her hair.

A neat parting to the side, she pushes her hair back and secures it with a French Tortoiseshell comb. Then places some curls on the other side with some pins and brushes out the back, curling it around her fingers tips and allowing it to drop naturally.

She stands up from the dressing table and puts on her pale pink silk petticoat. Then draws lines up the backs of her legs with eyeliner pencil.

She lifts her blue and white polka dot dress from the coat hanger on the wardrobe door, puts it on over her head, pulls it down and smooths it out.

A look in the mirror to make sure everything is hanging

nicely. She reaches for her brown peep-toe shoes and with the help of a shoehorn squeezes her feet into them.

A red and white polka dot scarf around her neck and a little flurry of artificial flowers as a broach pinned to her dress finishes her look.

She glances at the clock and picks up her brown handbag and waits by the lounge window.

The sound of a honking horn in the distance makes her lean forward and look out the side of the bay window. She smiles as a deep maroon Ford Convertible glides to a halt outside her house and an American soldier waves and pumps the horn again.

She grabs her brown handbag and hurries to open the front door.

"Hey babe, are you ready to jive?"

She laughs, closes the door and skips down the four steps where she rushes into his waiting arms.

"Yes, soldier I truly am." She says as she attempts a Southern American accent.

"I'm ready, willing and able."

"Let's go then honey. Can't wait."

The American soldier holds her hand, helps her into the car, and closes the door behind her as she settles into her seat.

They smile at each other as he starts the engine and the car smoothly moves forward.

"What song shall we sing?"

"Well, I've been listening to my seventy-eight while I was getting ready, so how about Chattanooga Choo Choo?"

"I love that one."

They sing, and sway and smile as they drive along. Song, after song, after song. They are not aware of the miles they have covered.

"Oh, look, we're here. That was quick." She says.

"Yes, I'll just park this old jalopy and then we can make our way to the beer tent, if you like."

"That would be lovely."

They park the car, make their way to the entrance, pay the entry fee and head for the beer tent.

"What will it be?"

"A small shandy will do please."

"I'll have a beer. Would you like to find a seat and I'll bring it over?"

"Yes, look, there's one in the corner there."

They sit together fondly looking into each other's eyes.

She fidgets with her neckerchief and broach.

"Shall we wander and take a look around? He says as he takes her hand.

They stroll arm in arm and view the side stalls. Clothing for sale. Wool for knitting with demonstrators showing off their craft.

Second-hand wares. Shoes. Everything anyone ever wanted for their country pursuits, rifles, hats, bags, brogues, jackets, caps, waterproofs.

Charity stalls, The British Red Cross and The Salvation Army. He puts a small donation in the tub. She buys a raffle ticket and wins a bar of fine soap.

"Ah, that reminds me." He says. "I've got something for you."

"What is it?" She says as her eyes light up.

He pulls out a bar of chocolate from his pocket, followed by a pair of silk stockings and some candy."

She laughs.

He smiles.

They kiss.

"I don't believe this; you are so thoughtful. What a crazy pair we are."

They embrace again and begin walking past the stalls once more, arm in arm.

"Shall we have something to eat?" He asks.

"Yes, I think we'd better have something as we'll need all our energy for this evening."

"What will it be then?"

"I've spied a good old English Fish and Chips van. Look over there." She points in the distance.

They run and laugh and buy their fish and chips.

"Wow I am so full up now." He says as he pulls on his trouser belt.

"Me too." She says as she pats her stomach.

They stroll about enjoying each other's company and looking at the exhibits at the event.

"Okay then babe. Time to swing and jive the night away."

He takes her hand and they run across the field to the tent where a band is just setting up. They sit at a table, excitement is brewing, the air is electric.

The trombonist gives a loud blast.

A man walks over to the microphone and taps it.

"Are you ready folks, ready to dance the night away? Forget about the war and your troubles. It's New Year's Eve, tomorrow it will be 1945, LET'S DANCE."

The band strikes up. People rise from their seats.

He takes her hand and they dance.

They twist and turn and jive and gyrate to the music.

They dance and swing and boogie all night long.

*

She wakes up. It is easier to lift her head. She strains to see the patient in the bed next to her, propped up with three pillows. All she can see is bandages, no features. The person is reading a newspaper. The headlines say, 1918 THE LONG WAR IS OVER.

"You are not stuck where you are unless you decide to be." ~ Wayne W. Dyer

14

MEG TO THE RESCUE

"Mum." Paula called out.

"What is it?"

"I'm going for a run on the hills."

"Isn't it a bit late in the afternoon for that?"

"I won't be long. I'll be back before dusk, anyway I'm taking Meg, she can look after me."

"All right then but do be careful. I'll order a pizza when you get back and we can watch a movie."

"See you later Mum. Come on Meg, let's get your collar and lead on."

Meg wriggled with anticipation as Paula placed the collar around her maned neck. Outside the fresh scent of salt and seaweed had drifted in on the sea breeze, Paula breathed it in. The pair took a shortcut through the park and up the slight incline to the public footpath that led to The Downs.

"Free." Said Paula as she unclipped the lead from Meg's collar. Meg began sniffing in the newly mown grass as Paula quickened her pace using the walk to the foot of the hills as a warmup.

They soon reached the long, narrow public footpath that led to the hills above Capital Bay, Jade's favourite haunt. Paula avoided the squashed empty cans and other pieces of debris that littered the alleyway the smell from which was overpowering at times and made her cover her nose.

On top of The Downs about a dozen sheep were grazing on the short, lush grass intertwined with clumps of sweet-smelling Gorse and an array of wildflowers, Cowslips, Buttercups and Red Clover.

Paula kept to the narrow, worn footpath. Meg trotted on ahead.

About ten minutes had passed when Paula decided to break into a gentle trot.

"Come on Meg, stay close." She said as the Sheepdog came to her side.

Paula looked out across the hills at the lowering sun sparkling on the water. A breeze had got up and played with her hair sending it over her face, she brushed it off with her hands.

Paula was about to pick up pace when suddenly her steps were halted by something, she saw in front of her.

It looked like a white football.

She thought of kicking it for Meg to chase but then it moved. It moved upward and she could clearly see it was someone's head covered in bandages. Then a whole body appeared as if coming up from out of the ground. A body covered in bandages. Paula called Meg to her side and hid behind a Gorse bush.

Seconds later a second bandaged figure appeared as if coming up from a hole in the ground. Then a third. Paula counted twenty in all. They gathered in a bunch, looked around and proceeded to walk over the brow of the hill. Paula crouched and followed darting from bush to bush. The wind blew the stench of rotting flesh her way. Meg pricked her ears and her nose began to twitch. Paula covered her mouth in an attempt to stop herself throwing up.

From the brow of the small hillock she could see a dozen sheep with their bellies ripped open, their innards lying on the grass. The group of what she now perceived to be Zombies moving purposefully toward them.

"I think they're going to eat the sheep Meg. Come on girl it's time for you to put your sheep herding lessons into practice."

Paula took Meg by the collar and gently led her away from the gorse bush behind which they were hiding. Paula had got to stop the Zombies from eating the dead sheep and killing even more. She pointed toward the group and shouted.

"Fetch.' Meg ran hard to the right in a semi-circle, slowed, and then began creeping with her head down toward the group of Zombies. The first Zombie that had appeared and the tallest stopped in his tracks and put his arms out to stop the others. Then the group made threatening noises to Meg. Paula held her breath hoping Meg would succeed in rounding up the Zombies though what she would do with them afterwards Paula had no idea.

Meg's hackles went up making her look far bigger than she really was, and her eyes went into tiny slits. The Zombies turned tail and ran.

Suddenly a young man came tearing over the brow of the hill on his quad bike.

"Get your bloody dog off my sheep or I'll shoot it." He shouted.

"My dog is not on your sheep." Said Paula.

"Your dog has killed my sheep and I'm going to shoot it."

"No," screamed Paula "it was the Zombies."

"What Zombies?" Shouted the young man.

"Them. "Said Paula as she pointed to the group of Zombies now in full flight followed by Meg.

"Then get your bloody Zombies off my land and my sheep."

"It's not your land, it's common land." Said Paula.

"Get the bloody Zombies and your dog away from here."

"They're not my Zombies." Shouted Paula.

"Well they're certainly not mine either."

The young man drove his quad bike over to Paula.

"Where did those bloody Zombies come from then?"

"I watched them emerge from the hill. Said Paula.

Meg was still circling the group of Zombies, keeping the bewildered looking group away from the sheep.

"Keep your dog busy with them then." Said the young man as he drove a little closer to the group of Zombies and took out a lasso and caught them with his first shot and gathered them into a tight bunch.

As he did so the rope appeared to go right through them and pull off their bandages revealing their insides. Blood oozed from open wounds and Paula could see the heart of the tallest Zombie beating inside its blood covered rib cage.

The young man pulled his lasso tighter and the group gathered closer and then fell over like a pack of paper playing cards. They landed on the ground in a heap of blood and innards and their bandages flapped in the wind.

"I'm going to have to clear up this mess. I'll take away the bandages and leave the rotting flesh to the foxes and Buzzards." Said the young man.

Paula stood both in shock and in awe, her face ashen.

"Where did you learn to lasso like that?"

"Oh, I've just spent a month on a cattle ranch in Montana."

"You did a fantastic job." Said Paula.

"So did your dog. "Said the young man as he patted Meg. "What's her name?"

"Meg."

"And yours?"

"Paula."

"I'm John from Capital Bay farm, at the bottom of the Downs" He pointed to a small clump of buildings down in the valley.

"Look, would you like to meet up for a drink tonight?"

"Sorry but I promised mum I'd be home shortly after my run and we were having pizza and watching a movie."

"Tomorrow then?" Said John.

"Yes, I'd like that." Said Paula.

"Good. Now I'd better go and get my farm hand to give me a hand with these dead sheep. Hopefully your Meg has helped stop the cause of all the sheep deaths I've had here lately.

Well done Meg."

"I'll see you tomorrow then at The Witches Brew, in the village for a drink or two. Nine o'clock?"

"Yes, I'll look forward to that. Come on Meg, time to go home now."

15

SHARLA

Sharla hurried through the narrow pedestrian precinct of the town she'd moved into that morning. At nine o'clock, the shops were opening, sellers in the market sorting out their wares.

The stallholders greeting their neighbours and empty crates slamming against the ground made for various sounds that echoed off the tall buildings around the market-town square.

A cold wind whipped through the scene, sending discarded drink cans, scraps of paper, and empty boxes dancing along the pavement.

Sharla pulled her long woollen scarf higher up around her neck as she shivered in the crisp morning air.

Other than the stallholders, there were few people about. Those that were there turned their heads; their eyes followed her as she walked with purposeful strides in her thick, black boots.

A chill gust of wind caught the hem of her dark blue cape, lifting it to reveal the green satin lining and the thick auburn curls that cascaded down below her waist.

She strode on fully aware of those piercing looks entering her world, wondering where she had come from and was she friend or foe. Anyone would think she'd horns sticking out the top of her head, she felt, by how their icy stares followed her. Maybe they'd never seen such a fresh, freckled complexion, wide emerald eyes, and bright auburn hair carried by a tall, female stranger in town before.

Sharla passed the funeral parlour with its displays of coffins and headstones, the gift shop with rows and rows of personalised mugs-Barry, Brenda, Gregory, Georgina-no mug with the name Sharla on it.

She reached the butcher's shop with its display of sheepskins and myriads of sausages. She stepped inside, searching for real meat, but all she could see were pies and pasties.

"Yes?" A stout man with a ruddy complexion asked.

"A large joint of your best beef, please, about one kilo in weight."

The man's plump body shuffled off out the back of the store, returning with a stainless-steel tray on which sat two large joints of beef, glistening trickles of blood oozing out onto the tray. He tucked some greaseproof paper around one joint and placed it on the scales.

"Under or over?"

"Pardon?"

"Under or over? This one is over the kilo, the other one will be under, which is it to be?"

"Over, thank you."

"You're not from these parts, are you? I can tell by your accent."

"No, I'm from down south."

"Thought as much. You're a strange lot from the other side of the river."

"Are we?"

"Yes, you come here all the time thinking you can buy cheap housing and take our jobs, but you don't fit in with our ways, and so you leave again."

"Oh, well, maybe things will be different for me. I moved in this morning, and I plan to stay."

"Please yourself. Here's your receipt for the meat."

Sharla placed a note on the glass counter. The man crumpled it in the palm of his podgy hand; then his fat, purple fingers fiddled with the edges.

"Can never be sure." He said as he brought the note up to the light and examined it. "There's been a lot of forgeries circulating lately."

"Oh, well, this is one I made earlier," Sharla giggled. Her words made the shop assistant look up from under his bushy eyebrows, and with a grunt, he placed her change on the counter. Sharla gathered the coins in her slender hands, picked up the neatly wrapped joint, and left the shop. Weird people around here, she thought.

Sharla strolled about the precinct, trying to get her bearings and making a mental map.

To her right were several chemists, hairdressers, and fast food outlets. To her left a supermarket and before her a row of banks and estate agents. She strode on past the banks and came to a large lawned area with a circle of seats where she sat down.

In the far corner, by some bushes, a homeless man sat on a wooden bench, curled up at his feet, his muscular white dog lay on the moss-covered stone slabs. A group of young children laughed as they chased each other around a small play area while parents pushed their offspring on the swings.

Sharla looked at her watch. It was eleven-thirty. She was about to open up the parcel of meat when the dog strained on the end of a long piece of rope and dragged the homeless man over to her seat. The dog stood with braced legs, red tongue lolling, saliva dripping from its enormous jaws. The weathered man sat down with a sigh. Sharla slid nearer her end of the metal seat as the stench from the man made her retch.

"Have you got any money you can give me; I need a meal for me and my dog Nelson."

Sharla looked at the dog and thought if the thin piece of rope it was pulling on were to break, the dog would be at her piece of beef and have a full stomach. Feeling sorry for the tramp, she reached into her pocket.

"I'm not sure," Said Sharla as her slender, white hand pulled out the change the butcher had given her. She picked out two coins with her long purple fingernails and leaned toward the man, dropping the coins in his open hand, the other hand steadying the meat package on her lap.

The beggar curled his filthy fingers around the coins and took them to his lips and pretended to kiss them. Without warning, his dog lunged forward to the end of the rope.

"Get that dog away from me., Sharla screamed, her arms flailing. "I'm allergic to them."

"Get back here, Nelson, stop being a bad dog." Shouted the homeless man as he yanked on the rope and drew the dog slowly to his side.

On hearing the commotion, a crowd gathered. Someone asked Sharla if she was all right.

"Yes, I'm just allergic to dogs, that's all, and this dog tried to attack me."

"No, he didn't. He doesn't like strangers, that's all." Retorted the old man as he stood up and gathered his ragged coat around him. "My Nelson is harmless; it's you, it's because you're a foreigner in these parts."

By now, Sharla's eyes had become bloodshot and watery, the bright emerald green hardly visible. She began coughing and sneezing.

"Are you sure you're okay?' Asked a lone woman.

"Yes, I've got this allergy. That's all. It'll pass."

The weathered old man took his dog back to the wooden bench where they both sat, the man tutting for quite some time.

The children in the play area went back to the swings. Sharla looked at her watch again. It was noon.

She dabbed her eyes with a red handkerchief and reached into her pocket and pulled out a purple cloth that matched her fingernails. She spread the material on her lap and smoothed it out with the palms of her pale hands. Then placed the package of meat on top and began to unwrap it.

As she did so, the homeless man's dog Nelson began to bark furiously and lunge on the lead again. It was as much as the man could do to hold him back.

Sharla raised the slab of meat toward her face as she bent slightly forward. She looked across at the dog, and the crowd that had gathered, opened her mouth wide and sunk her ivory coloured fangs into the joint.

Her bloodshot eyes looked up under her auburn fringe, revealing a large expanse of the whites of her eyes that now gleamed with inbuilt devilry.

A sudden blast of freezing air whistled through the precinct, swirled through her auburn curls, revealing two white horns coming from the crown of her head.

As the people around her stood stunned, a little boy alighted from the swings and ran over.

"You've got horns sticking out the top of your head."

"I know," Said Sharla, that's because I'm a Shewolf."

"My dad is a Werewolf; would you like to meet him?"

"Yes, I'd like that," Said Sharla as she took the package of meat in one hand and gently grasped the little boy's out-stretched hand with the other. Together, in a puff of blue haze, they disappeared into the bushes behind the homeless man and his dog. The dog gave out an eerie whine, turned around three times, and curled up in a ball fast asleep within seconds.

16

HARRY'S HELL HOLE

*H*arry sat alone in the main office of The Brag newspaper, the glow from his desk lamp amplified the darkness surrounding him. He gazed out the window at the neon city below, his eyelids feeling heavier by the minute. Knowing another strong cup of coffee was not an antidote for lack of sleep he decided it was time to pack up and leave. He gathered together the files he'd been working on and with his forearm brushed them into his bag, zipped it up, put on his jacket and headed for home.

Each bulb in the long corridor leading to the elevator automatically turned on and off as he passed beneath it. The absence of night-time cleaning staff and security, due to company cutbacks added to the eeriness the low lights created.

Harry pushed the elevator down arrow and waited. The doors clanked open, he stepped inside relieved to finally be leaving the building after what had been a long exhausting week. Spending the weekend recuperating and catching up on odd jobs in the garden were now high on his agenda.

Harry leaned against the cold metal wall stared at the floor and waited for the elevator to move. It gave a few shudders, the main lights flickered, then the burring sounds told him he was going downwards.

Harry rubbed his eyes, closed them and waited. The elevator, being as old as the dilapidated building in which it sat, was generally slow and would take a while to go from the thirty fourth floor to the basement level where his car was parked.

Suddenly there was a grinding noise, the main lighting was extinguished. For a few seconds he was surrounded by complete darkness then the emergency strip bulb lit up.

"What the bloody hell. That's all I need."

Harry pressed the ground floor button and as the elevator did not respond he pressed all the buttons and then kicked the doors. After the sounds of metal against metal had subsided there was silence. He took out his mobile phone but there was no signal. He tried the elevator emergency alarm button, which was not lit, and nothing happened when he touched it.

He looked up at the flickering secondary lighting, "Now don't you dare give way on me." He said.

Harry put his ear to the elevator doors in the hope of hearing signs of life outside. There were none. Neither were there any mechanical noises that might indicate the elevator was about to start up again. The only sound was the air conditioning and that appeared to be labouring somewhat. Harry tried his mobile phone again, pressing the buttons for 911 but there was no response. He slowly slid down to the floor placed his head in his hands and looked at the time on his phone.

"Ten minutes. Ten bloody minutes I've been in this shitty hole. I could be halfway home by now."

He sighed, stood up, went over to the doors and tried to get his fingers into the slit between them in order to pull them apart but to no avail. Feeling powerless he kicked the doors and then pressed all the buttons several times.

"Move, dam you, move." He shouted.

Harry was beginning to feel hot, he undid his tie, took off his jacket and threw it on the floor. He stood in the silence, listening, realising the air-conditioning was no longer working he began to panic. Once again, he tried putting his fingers into the tiny gap between the metal doors. He took out his car keys and managed to wedge one into the slit, but the key twisted out of shape and did little to help open the doors. He threw the bunch of keys at the wall; they made a sharp cracking sound as metal hit metal. Crouching down he ran his hands through his hair wondering what on earth he was going to do to get himself out of such a mess. No-one would come to the office now until about six o'clock Monday morning when the cleaners began working. He wouldn't survive till then, not with the air-conditioning out of action, he felt as if he were being stifled and just longed for some fresh air.

After a few minutes Harry bent over, reached out to the corner of the floor and yanked at the carpet. He pulled the carpet away and felt for a trap door but there was none. He looked around the walls, the air-conditioning vent was small, no use in trying to escape through that unless he could shrink to the size of a mouse, he thought.

Harry stretched up on tip toes to the corner of the ceiling. He could just reach the shiny mirrored panelling. He pulled at the corner and it came away along with a ton of dust that got in his eyes and started him coughing. Better be careful, he thought as he exposed a number of wire cables. Luckily the emergency bulb was still working, and he could see what he was doing. Harry was elated to find what he supposed was a trap door, big enough for a man to fit through, in the roof of the elevator.

"It's got to be an exit." He said as the seriousness of his situation hit him. He was becoming very thirsty and began coughing again as he felt as if a lump was developing in his throat.

Jumping up several times and stretching as high as he could, he managed to turn each lever. With the final jump he pushed the trap door and it flew up in the air and landed with a clank on the elevator roof. Immediately fresh air whooshed inside. Harry stood still, looked up and breathed in the delightful blast of freshness.

He looked around the elevator as if expecting a chair or ladder to appear from no-where. He grabbed his bag, placed it beneath the opening, stood on it and reached up as high as he could. He felt a tiny lip around one edge and clung onto it with his fingertips, but he could not get enough leverage in order to pull all his weight up through the escape hatch.

He tried again only this time he put one foot on the small ledge afforded by the framed poster of someone enjoying a skiing holiday in the Alps. This tiny ledge allowed him to push up further and then swing one leg up and into the hole. It reminded him of the move he made when pole vaulting for the team at University. He then swung the other leg up and managed to wriggle his whole body through the gap.

Although he was tired, he felt a rush of adrenalin. There was a metal ladder on the exterior wall. He placed his hands on it as he looked up and saw a tiny speck of light in the distance. He began to climb. Nearer and nearer the speck of daylight came as his lungs heaved with the strain of climbing.

Suddenly there were noises so loud he had to wrap his arms around the ladder and block up his ears. The ladder began to vibrate. Harry looked down and could see the elevator was moving, although slowly. He watched for a while wondering if it would come right up to him, but it appeared to go up and then down and back up again. It was then that he realised the internal computer had probably registered all the buttons he'd pressed earlier and was carrying out the requests. Then the elevator finally went down and seemed to disappear from view.

Harry began to climb again toward the speck of light that was now much brighter. He was getting closer to it. Maybe it was a way out, he thought, and this thought spurred him on faster.

Finally, he reached the light, exhausted. There was a tiny platform, big enough to get his feet onto. He stood on it and peeped through the small square of glass to the outside world. In the distance he could just make out the backs of two fire officers who were standing near an open door. Realising that he too was standing at a door he looked for a handle but there was none.

"Dam it, the bloody thing opens from the outside."

Then he began to shout and bang on the window. He kicked the door and screamed.

"Hey, hey, help, let me out of here." His cries went unheard and the two firemen disappeared into the dark doorway.

Harry hung onto a metal pole near the top of the ladder and flopped down onto the step and began to cry. Thoughts of ending his days locked in this hell hole and people finding a dead body, rushed through his mind.

As weary as he was, he decided to climb back down. Maybe an elevator door would open as he reached a floor. Maybe the elevator would come back up. Maybe... He couldn't think of any more maybe's, he just continued to climb slowly back down the cold metal ladder.

A beam of light shone on his head.

A voice above shouted, "Hey you mister, what are you doing in here?"

Harry looked up but was blinded by the light, never-the-less he gained new momentum and began climbing back up the ladder. Someone reached out a hand and he grabbed it and felt the strength of the person pulling him to safety.

"You're all right now mate. You're safe."

Harry collapsed in a heap.

"Thank you."

"Can someone call for the Air Ambulance?" Shouted the fire officer.

"What time is it?" Asked Harry as he shielded his eyes from the bright sunlight.

"Ten AM. How long have you been in that elevator shaft?"

"That makes it about twelve hours then, since Friday night."

"It's Sunday mate. You've been in there a lot longer than twelve hours. We're getting you help now. The Air Ambulance is on its way."

"Thank you, thank you. I've always wanted to go in an Air Ambulance but preferably as a pilot and not as a patient. Said Harry as he lay back on the stretcher provided by the two firemen and went unconscious.

17

IT'S WIN, WIN

Bret stood by the basement elevator, his finger hovering over the up button. Discreetly he watched Mrs. Montgomery get out of her car and reach over the driver's seat for her handbag and some files. He amused himself by thinking how shapely her legs looked in high heels and how her hips swayed rhythmically as she walked toward him smiling.

"Mr. Sheridan isn't it?"

"Yes, Mrs Montgomery. I've pressed the button."

"Oh, well we'll probably have to wait ages, she sighed, "the lift has been very temperamental of late. I see you managed to get here before the storm hit. My car is soaked I'm going to call on a staff member to wipe it down for me. Ah, look the elevator's arrived at last."

Bret indicated with his hand for Mrs. Montgomery to enter first.

"Twenty-six, is it, the same as me?"

"Yes, thank you Mr. Sheridan., although I'd much rather be sunbathing on some Caribbean island than helping Jack out today. I find it so tedious. I notice you don't find the work here boring Mr. Sheridan. I have long," She hesitated, "Jack and I have long admired your work. You've been here about five years, now haven't you?"

"Yes, Mrs. Montgomery, five years last week."

"Well, in that case I think we should be on first name terms. Bret isn't it? I'm Emma, which I'm sure you know."

"Yes," Bret cleared his throat as he replied.

"Well I do hope this storm doesn't last long as I need to be getting off early this afternoon."

"Oh, I'm sure it will soon be over and done with."

Suddenly the elevator came to a shaky halt, the main light went out and the emergency light flickered above.

"That's all I need Bret. Just my luck. I bet it's the storm causing a power cut again. It happened last month, and the power was off for over twenty minutes. It gets so hot in these elevators when this happens."

"I'm sure the power will come back on soon, Emma. There's not a lot we can do about it at the moment."

Bret stared at the floor while listening for any mechanical sound that might indicate the elevator was moving again all he could hear were his and Emma's breathing. The emergency light flickered a few times and then the elevator was in complete darkness.

"Great, now the emergency lighting has decided to pack in. We'll just have to stand here in the dark and twiddle our thumbs." Bret said as he lost all sense of space in the blackness.

Bret stepped back and leaned against the cold metal wall his eyes searching for any single ray of light but there was none.

"I don't like the dark at all Bret. I find it quite threatening."

"You'll be all right Emma. Come and stand over here, maybe you'll feel better if you stand nearer to me."

Bret felt a hand on his arm and then Emma's shoe bumped his. He was thinking he didn't mean that close.

"We can't exactly play, I spy with my little eye," Bret tried to laugh.

"No Bret but I know what we can play." Said Emma as her hand reached down to Bret's left buttock.

Bret coughed.

"I'm sure the power will be off for quite some time Bret; in any case we could even press the disable button and keep it standing here a lot longer If we so wished."

"I'm not quite sure what you mean Emma."

Emma's hand crept around to the front of Bret's trousers. "I mean this," she said as she firmly placed one hand on his crotch and the other began to unzip his trousers.

"But what will Mr. Montgomery, say?"

"Jack isn't here, it's just you and me and the elevator. Come on Bret, relax, don't you like to have some fun once in a while."

"Yes, but."

It was too late. Emma had her skirt up and panties down and was pulling Bret to the floor and on top of her as if she were an expert at seduction.

Bret felt Emma's hands squeezing his buttocks, her nails digging into his flesh. A few thrusts and it was all over. Emma pushed Bret to one side, he rolled over onto the carpeted floor. Sounds of clothing being adjusted came from somewhere in the elevator but Bret still felt disorientated by the blackness.

The emergency light lit up again illuminating Bret's bare backside like a beam from a police helicopter exposing his guilt. Whatever had come over him, he thought, it wasn't as if he were flying at high altitude or a member of The Mile-High Club, somehow Emma and the stuck elevator had affected him in a way he never knew possible.

"Come on Bret, the elevator will be working again in a minute, get yourself organised." Said Emma as she smoothed out her skirt. Bret jumped up, tucked his shirt back into his trousers and was just doing up his zip and belt when the elevator door opened revealing Mr. Montgomery who was standing beneath the twenty-sixth-floor sign. His eyes seemed to bore right through Bret.

"There you are darling I was so worried about you. Nigel messaged me to say he'd seen you enter the lift when the power extinguished. I know how you hate lifts at the best of times. Are you all right darling?"

"Yes, of course dear. No need to fret. Bret kindly entertained us both with I spy with my little eye." Said Emma as she took her husband's arm.

"Well done Bret, Mr. Sheridan and thank you for taking care of my wife. Now Emma you do look rather flushed, were you at all frightened?"

"No, it was quite warm in there that's all. Can we go to your office now I could do with a strong coffee?"

"Of course."

Bret watched the pair trot off down the corridor as he headed for his own office.

Bret sat at his desk wiping his brow with his handkerchief and contemplating the morning's events when the phone on his desk rang, He picked it up.

"Sheridan, in my office-NOW."

Bret walked briskly down the long corridor to Mr. Montgomery's office, somehow it seemed to take longer than usual as his feet felt like lumps of lead. He tapped the door.

"Enter. Sheridan, my wife tells me you, comforted her while the pair of you were in the lift."

"I tried to help her relax as she said she was afraid she might feel a bit claustrophobic, sir."

"That's what you call it is it? My wife, Mrs. Montgomery tells me it was a bit more than that. To be quite honest Sheridan I'm somewhat surprised by your behaviour. A young man like yourself. How old are you-twenty-five?"

"Twenty-two, sir."

"Twenty-two! Well that surprises me even more. I wouldn't have thought you were into that sort of thing."

"What sort of thing sir?"

"You know exactly what I'm talking about Sheridan. Mrs. Montgomery has told me everything. We have no secrets you know."

"It was Emma, Mrs. Montgomery, who came on to me sir. I just, went with the flow."

"Now look here lad, I've got two propositions to put to you. I frown upon this kind of behaviour at Montgomery Logistics and I will have no more of it on these premises. Do you hear boy?"

"Yes, sir."

"I'm going to offer you two alternatives and I'm sure I know which one you will take. The first is that you make sure you leave this building with all your belongings by close of business today and without any references."

"But sir, it was Mrs. Montgomery."

"Stop interrupting me boy. You leave today, without any references or you come to our country house once a week to entertain my wife. I hope you get my meaning lad."

"Yes, I do sir."

"Well, what is it going to be? Entertain my wife, and you must be broad minded for that, or leave your position without any references from this company. Which is it boy? Come on, out with it, I haven't got time to waste."

"I'll leave right now sir. I'll gather my belongings and leave right now." Said Bret as he turned toward the door.

"Hang on a minute Sheridan, Bret, I thought I'd made you a jolly good offer. Don't you like my wife, Mrs. Montgomery, Emma? She's a lovely girl, some five years younger than me and great fun to be with, I'm sure you'll get along perfectly don't you think."

"No sir, I don't think. I'd prefer to leave now if that's all right with you."

"Please yourself lad. I'll get my secretary to escort you out of the building. Mrs. Montgomery will be rather disappointed with your decision, it's not often that she's shunned by people like you."

Bret followed the secretary from the room, sweat bubbles appeared on his forehead. He quickly gathered all his belongings from his office, placed them in a box and took the elevator to the underground car park. The lift worked perfectly this time.

At basement level he placed the box of belongings on the driver's seat, took out his notebook and mobile phone. He pressed the buttons and waited for the dialling tone.

"Oh, hi, It's Mr. Sheridan, Bret Sheridan, I'm just phoning to let you know I'll accept that job you offered me yesterday. When can I start?"

18

DYING WISH

"I'm writing my will out Donna."

Veronica sat at her dining room table her arthritic fingers struggling to hold the pen. I placed her spare door key on the table and pulled up a chair alongside her.

"Would you like me to help you? Although I guess I'm not supposed to look at what you're writing." I said.

"No, that's all right. You can look, so long as you're not a beneficiary. I'm trying to decide who should inherit half my house. I could offer it to you. I'm not sure what to do with it. I'm certainly not letting my sister Mavis have it all."

"I don't want half your house Veronica; I've got my own." I said, while secretly wishing she'd leave everything she owned to me.

"I've decided, after a great deal of thought, to leave one half to my friend Julie. Mavis isn't going to like that one bit. Neither is her boyfriend Reg."

"What you put in your will is your business Veronica and none of theirs."

"I know but Mavis says Julie is only after my money since I gave her a cheque for three hundred pounds. Julie's daughter passed her degree and I was so pleased for them both I wrote out a cheque for her. Mavis says I should phone Julie up and tell her I want the money back. I can't do that, after all it was a gift and I was pleased to be able to give it to her."

I placed an arm around Veronica's shoulders as she began to sniffle.

"The vicar came around the other day," Veronica continued. "He said the church needed a new window at the back and it would cost over two hundred pounds. I gave him a cheque for four hundred to cover everything. Mavis was fine about that, but she went crazy when she saw the stub for Julie's money. Reg has now taken my cheque book with him and says I can't write out any more cheques without asking them first. They both said they would leave me a twenty pound note each day in case I wanted to pop to the corner shop for anything. They've also taken my bank cards. I'm very upset about it Donna."

I didn't know what to say to comfort Veronica and didn't want to get mixed up in a family row.

"I'm sure they have your best interests at heart Veronica," I said, "You've contributed a great deal to the church over the years haven't you."

"Yes, I have Donna. But now because I was left with a good pension after Harry died and because we didn't have any children people think I'm worth a fortune and I'm not." Veronica dabbed her eyes with her lace trimmed handkerchief as she became more distressed.

"Here let me get you a glass of water and then I'll help you finish the will."

I went into the sunlit kitchen and poured some bottled fizzy water-Veronica's favourite.

"Now drink up and then I'll make us both a nice cup of tea."

I'd only been back in the kitchen a few minutes when I heard Veronica begin to wail.

"Whatever is the matter?" I asked

"Mavis came around yesterday and said she doesn't want to have anything to do with my money and so now Reg has got Power of Attorney. They said they decided to do it before I went…before I went…"

Veronica was trying hard to speak but the words would not come out.

"Went where Veronica? Please tell me what has been going on with you, Mavis and Reg."

"Before I went senile."

I was taken aback at Mavis' comments about her sister as she appeared to have all her faculties. Her only ailments were her arthritis and stomach ulcer, for which she was being treated by the doctor. We'd had some wonderful conversations whenever I'd come around for a short visit. I was appalled at the idea anyone could say Veronica was going senile.

"Come on, drink your tea Veronica," was all I could say.

"I've made an appointment with the solicitors in the high street for tomorrow. Would you be kind enough as to help me get there Donna?"

"Of course, Veronica. No problem." I said. "I'll come around first thing in the morning and help you get ready and then take you in the wheelchair. It's too far for you to walk and there's no parking outside."

"Please don't tell Mavis or Reg if you happen to see them." Said Veronica as she sniffled again.

"I promise I won't say a thing. Now drink your tea up and let me put this document somewhere safe for you. I placed the document in the bottom of Veronica's writing bureau while noticing the twenty-pound note tucked underneath the photo of her and Harry. What a sad situation, I thought to myself but decided it was none of my business what went on between Veronica and her sister.

The following morning, I arrived early and let myself in with the spare key. Veronica was watching the news channel as usual. She already had on her hat, coat and outdoor shoes.

"Shall I make you a cup of tea Veronica before we go. It's a bit early for your appointment."

"No, I'm fine Donna. I've been up for hours. I got myself ready and I've had a slice of toast. We can go as soon as you get the wheelchair out for me."

I unfolded the wheelchair and Veronica steadied herself with her walking stick and then lowered herself onto the seat. Her body looked frail, but her mind certainly was not. Pushing the wheelchair on the thick carpet was rather difficult but we were soon outside, and the going was much better.

"It's a beautiful day Veronica."

"Yes, it is. The sun is very warm. Let's go the long way around as you said we were a bit early for my appointment. I pointed the wheelchair down the hill and sauntered along trying to waste time. Veronica hadn't been outside the house for at least a month and I thought the sunshine would do her good. We got to the bottom of the road, turned right and then turned right again. The going was hard now as it was uphill.

"We're nearly there," I puffed between breaths, thinking I would be glad to sit down once we were inside the solicitor's office.

I put the brake on the wheelchair and was just about to open the solicitor's door when someone grabbed my arm.

"And where do you think you're going Donna with my sister?"

It was Mavis and her side kick, Reg.

"She's taking me to see the solicitor. I'm making my will out today." Said Veronica.

"But we planned to come and help you do that Veronica." Mavis said.

"Yes and try and get me to leave everything to you. Well I'm not going to. I'm leaving half my house to Julie."

"But Julie's your cleaner. How can you leave your house to your cleaner?" asked Mavis.

"Quite easily." Replied Veronica with a toss of her head.

"I suppose you put her up to this didn't you Donna." Said Mavis as she wagged a finger in my face.

"Now don't you bring me into this. All I'm doing is helping Veronica keep her appointment with the solicitor."

"And who made the appointment-you?"

"No, Veronica did it all on her own."

"But she's not capable. She's got dementia. We're going to have her certified." Said Mavis

My jaw dropped on hearing those words from Veronica's sister. How hateful, I thought.

Veronica began howling and struggled to undo the seat belt of the wheelchair.

"I'll show you who's senile and got dementia dear sister." Said Veronica as she stood up and leaned toward the door handle of the solicitor's office just as the solicitor himself opened it from the other side. Veronica fell forward and landed in the doorway.

"Oh, my goodness. Are you hurt Veronica?" I asked as I helped the solicitor pick her up and get her back onto her feet. We brushed her coat down. She looked a bit pale and shaken but otherwise she appeared all right.

"I'm fine. Just a little tumble and I've had a few of those lately."

Meanwhile Mavis, who was now quite red in the face and Reg, who was wearing his usual blank expression, just stood watching and did not lift a finger to help Veronica.

Veronica turned to Mavis and Reg. "Go home and leave me alone. I'm on official business and I don't want to be disturbed."

"I'll talk to you later." Said Mavis as she once again wagged a finger in my face. "And you sister dear, I will see you later as well and you had better make sure Julie is not mentioned in that will or I'll see to it that you're taken straight to the hospital and admitted."

Mavis stormed off with Reg trailing along behind.

"Do come in Veronica and …?"

"Donna. I'm Mavis' next-door neighbour." I said.

"Ah, pleased to meet you." Said the solicitor. "Take a seat over there. Are you sure you're all right Veronica? Would you like a cup of tea?"

"No, I'm fine thank you. I just want to get this business over and done with."

I made myself comfortable on a chair by the window where I could look out over the pretty garden. I tried to be as unobtrusive as possible.

After about an hour the solicitor called in two members of his staff and they witnessed Veronica's signature on her will. It was all done.

"I'm ready to go now Donna." Veronica said as she turned to look at me.

"I'll go and fetch your wheelchair." I left the room thinking Veronica looked rather pale. Maybe the whole episode with her sister and Reg and falling over had shaken her up a bit.

"I've done it Donna. I'm glad it's all finished now and legal." Veronica said.

"I'm happy for you. Now let's get you home." I said as I wheeled the chair the short way back to Veronica's home.

"So, Julie is your cleaner. I've never met her."

"She was my cleaner, many years ago. Then Mavis said I had to get rid of her and use her cleaner instead. But we've stayed friends. It's about thirty years now. She's like the daughter I never had. I'm so pleased I've sorted that will out. Goodness knows what Mavis and Reg are going to say, but I'm not scared of them."

"Come on Veronica, let's get you home." I said.

Once outside Veronica's property I helped her back inside and into her chair and then switched on the tv. The news channel again.

"Shall I make you a cup of tea Veronica?'

"No, I'm fine. I just want to rest now. It's been a rather trying day. I'll get myself some tea shortly after I've rested.

The following morning, I was getting dressed and ready to pop around to see if Veronica had got over the previous day's trauma when I noticed Mavis and Reg get out of their car and an ambulance turn up. After a few minutes the ambulance drove off again.

I went outside and found Mavis crying into her handkerchief.

"What's up?" I asked. "Has something happened to Veronica?"

"She pressed her emergency buzzer early this morning but when the paramedics came, she was already dead, and they could not resuscitate her. They think her ulcer had burst. They said they cannot take a dead body in the ambulance and so we are waiting for a hearse to collect her.

"I'm so sorry to hear that Mavis." I said and went back into my own home thinking how glad I was that Veronica managed to get her will signed and sealed in time. No-one could have known she would pass away like that. Maybe it was the fall at the solicitor's office. Maybe it was the argument with Mavis. Who knows, but she got her dying wish.

19

STILL WAITING

Jenny and I had been seeing each other for over three years when finally, she agreed to let me meet her family. But if I'd known how the day was going to turn out then I might have left them all as anonymous beings in the background.

We were invited to Sunday lunch and arrived mid-morning. I parked the car in the sweeping driveway of the large, Tudor style country residence. It's got to be at least six bedrooms, I thought as I gazed up at the impressive, vine covered walls. The garden was immaculate. I thought of the humble terraced house of my parents I'd moved out of three years earlier.

Coughing nervously, I followed Jenny to the front door which was opened by her father. He shook my hand and pointed me toward the kitchen where I greeted Jenny's mother with another warm handshake and a small kiss on the cheek.

"Would you like a cup of tea? Ben, isn't it? You can call me Sylvia."

"Yes, thanks, Sylvia." I smiled and wondered what to do next or where to go.

"Come into the living room Ben and chat with Dad." Jenny called from the hallway. I smiled at Mr Johnson as I entered and wondered which of the three sofas to sit on.

"Everyone around here calls me Fred. Short for Frederick."

I smiled again and sat down when Fred pointed to the largest sofa by the window. Sylvia entered with a tray of tea and biscuits.

"Milk and sugar Ben?"

"Yes, both thanks."

I had just finished drinking my tea and eating a couple of biscuits when I saw a shiny black car shoot up the long drive and park outside the giant bay window. I thought the girl sitting in the passenger seat looked familiar. Then to my horror I saw that it was Rosemary from the office. Rosemary who I'd dated a few times over the past year. I nearly dropped my cup and saucer as I fumbled to put them back on the tray.

"Would you like another Ben?" Sylvia asked

"No thanks. I'm fine." I hoped my unease would not show. Could Rosemary be discreet and not tell anyone of our recent encounters, I wondered as I turned around to face the door.

"Ah here comes Rosemary and Shaun. They make such a lovely couple." Said Sylvia.

Meanwhile Jenny and her father had gone to the front door to let Rosemary and Shaun in.

I stood up and let my right-hand play with the car keys in my pocket as I admired the black saloon parked in the middle of the gravel drive. My left hand grasped the phone in my other pocket as I recalled the tantalising texts Rosemary and I had shared over the past year.

Footsteps on the wooden floor caused me to turn and see Rosemary enter, followed by Shaun, Jenny and her father.

Jenny came straight over to me. "Ben I'd like you to meet my darling sister Rosemary and her beau, Shaun." I was sure there was a hint of sarcasm in Jenny's voice. Rosemary kept a straight face as she shook my hand.

"Pleased to meet you Ben, at last. Jenny has spoken of you often. This is my boyfriend Shaun. We've only known each other for a couple of months but we get on very well, don't we?" Rosemary turned to Shaun as he nodded while reaching to shake my hand.

"Yes, I love Rosemary's sense of humour." Shaun said.

I do too, I thought, and her looks. Jenny was a little plainer than the shapely Rosemary and rather immature at times, but the relationship suited me. We'd had a fling at University and then it just seemed to continue from that. Jenny moved in with me. We went on holiday together. We went to the cinema together. We enjoyed each other's company. Rosemary was so different. She was fun loving, vivacious, curvy and I was captivated by her the first day she came to work at the newspaper offices as chief journalist.

She knew I had a long-term partner. I had explained that we were more like friends than lovers. Rosemary had never mentioned a boyfriend to me.

"Well now you've all met each other I'm going to get the lunch organised. Who's going to come into the kitchen and help?" Asked Sylvia. Jenny, her father and Shaun followed immediately. I stayed behind with Rosemary.

"You didn't tell me you had a sister." I whispered

"You never asked." Said Rosemary as she glanced toward the kitchen to see if anyone was looking.

"Anyway, you haven't got the same surname, so how was I to know you were Jenny's sister?"

"I'm a journalist, remember? I'm also an author and I like to go by my pseudonym. Besides you'd always been honest about your long-term girlfriend. There's little I can do to grab your attention and get you to leave her. Jenny has always come out trumps no matter what she does. I've always had to struggle for whatever I wanted."

"You don't have to struggle with me Rosemary. I'd willingly leave Jenny if you ever gave a hint that you wanted a full-on relationship."

"Come on everyone, into the dining room. Dinner is being served." Sylvia called from the kitchen.

Rosemary and I left the conversation there, tried to look nonchalant and went in to eat lunch. The meal looked and smelled delicious, but I had lost my appetite.

"So, when are you two love birds going to tie the knot?" Sylvia looked straight at me as she asked a question I was not expecting. I began to snicker as I almost choked on a roast potato.

"Oh, we're young yet." Sylvia. "Plenty of time." Jenny kicked my shin under the table.

"Shaun and I are getting married, Mum and Dad." Rosemary blurted out to everyone's surprise. "That's one reason why we came over today. To let you know. We're going to have a baby. Or rather I'm going to have a baby and Shaun knows he's not the father as he's been found to be infertile. He's agreed to bring the child up as his own."

Sylvia, Fred, Jenny and I stopped with our knives and forks in mid-air as we listened to this news.

"But wouldn't you want to marry the father?" I found myself asking Rosemary.

Rosemary's eyes became large as she fixed a stare in my direction. "You always said you didn't want children Ben. From the day we first met when I came into your office you told me you didn't want any children."

I could not believe what Rosemary had just come out with. How could she burst out with this in front of Jenny and her parents and even Shaun?

"You know each other?" Jenny asked as she pushed her chair back and stood up. "You already know my sister? You've been seeing her behind my back? You bastard. And now she is going to have your bastard child."

"Look Jenny," I said. "It's not like that."

"What is it like then Ben?" Asked Sylvia as she leaned over the table toward me.

"Rosemary and I had a fling once, that's all. I've been faithful to Jenny all the time."

"Faithful! Faithful! Is getting my sister pregnant being faithful?" Jenny screamed in my face.

"Rosemary, I'll marry you. Get rid of Shaun. I want to marry you. I love you. I want to be with you and our child." I shouted.

"I can't believe what I'm hearing here Ben Michaels. You always told me we were too young to get married and you didn't want any children. You hypocrite." Jenny said as she poured her red wine over my head and stormed out of the room. I heard her crying as she stomped up the stairs.

"What is this all about Ben and Rosemary? Is this true? Are you expecting Ben's child?"

"Yes Mum. I thought it was a fling. I knew he was living with Jenny all these years and I didn't want to break up their relationship."

"Well you seem to have done a really good job of that

without even trying. How could you get yourself pregnant in this day and age? Why could you not have been careful?"

"It's all my fault Sylvia. We went away for the weekend and Rosemary said she had forgotten to bring her pills with her."

"I think you'd better leave Ben and never come back. We don't want the likes of you around here."

"Now, now Sylvia don't be too harsh on the lad. These things happen and we can sort it out somehow." Fred said.

"No, we can't I want him out of the house *NOW* and I never want to see his face here again. He's not only ruined Jenny's life but he's also ruined Rosemary's life."

Sylvia grabbed me by the elbow and pulled me along to the front door. She then opened the door, shoved me through it and slammed it behind me. I was at a loss. What could I do?

I stood by my car and as I opened the door, I could see Jenny's tearstained face at her bedroom window and Rosemary's red-eyed face staring at me through the ground floor bay window. What a mess, I thought.

I drove down the long, tree-lined drive wishing I'd never persuaded Jenny to let me meet her parents.

At the end of the drive I stopped the car, got out my phone and sent a text to Rosemary. "Will you marry me?" I asked. I'm still waiting for the reply.

20

THE TIGERS

My brother's toys were always better than mine. He had an electric train set. It was enormous. Dad built it for him. It filled our conservatory. I loved to watch the trains go around, through the tunnels at each end, past the two stations either side and back around again. Roger, that's my brother's name, used to stop the goods train and fill it up with coal, hay bales and cattle and then move the various trains into their sidings. It looked so much fun.

I wasn't allowed to touch it. I did once, when everyone was in the garden and the train derailed and I got told off. Dad would let me switch it on sometimes, but that's all. I could only watch them both, Dad and Roger, getting so much enjoyment from it. How I longed to make the signals go up and down. How I dreamed one day of putting the Station Master on another platform. My fingers itched to pick up the little old lady and the Jack Russel Terrier and place them near the Ticket Office.

Roger also had metal toy trucks, lorries, and wagons that once belonged to Granddad. Plus, a farmyard with all kinds of farm animals. I wasn't allowed to play with these either. One day, when Roger was busy in his bedroom, I took his metal lorry out of the box, opened up the two doors at the back and put some cows inside it. Then I pushed it up and down and made engine noises. Roger said he knew I'd been tampering with the lorry as it now had a scratch on one of the doors at the back.

My toys were dolls-loads of them, and a teddy bear I called Virginia. I loved Virginia but I hated the dolls. They didn't do anything. Roger's train went around and around the track and you could push his lorries up and down, my dolls just sat there in the cot and did nothing, except they opened and shut their eyes. Virginia could growl like a real bear but in order to get her to do it you had to squeeze her tummy very hard. I would lay her on her back and wait for the sound of a clonk. Then I would squeeze her tummy and slowly put her on her front. Baa-she would go and then another clonking sound. Eventually she stopped making any noises at all.

One day a miracle happened. My sister became ill and was covered in spots. Mum said I couldn't go near her. We slept in the same bedroom and the day Karen got sick I had to sleep on the sofa in the lounge so that I didn't come out in spots. The real miracle was when Mum told me I had to play with Roger; *had to,* there was no getting away from it and Roger had no say in the matter. I was jumping up and down with joy. I could play with his train set, his lorries and farm animals and all his other toys-yippee!

I went over to Roger that morning and told him what Mum had said. He didn't say much except that he and Harry were going to spend the day as Tigers and girls weren't allowed to be Tigers.

I asked why not but Roger didn't have an answer for that. Then Harry said he would initiate me. I asked him what initiate meant and he said he wanted some of my blood. That frightened me a bit, but I thought I had to obey Mum's orders as Karen was sick in bed.

I asked Harry how he was going to get a bit of my blood and he produced a pen knife. He said he would cut his finger, Roger's finger and my finger, and we would have to mix all our blood together and smother it on our foreheads. I felt as if I was going to be sick.

Just then Mum came into the conservatory where we were sitting underneath the train set. She peeped at us and told us to make sure we all played nicely together, and we were not to disturb her as she was busy looking after Karen. She said she'd made some sandwiches and we could go down to the beach and eat them there. We sat still, trying to look as if we were being as good as possible and nodded to Mum.

When Mum was out of sight, I stuck my finger out at Harry and he tried to cut it but the blade must have been blunt and nothing happened. I winced all the same. Then Roger said we could just pretend by putting our fingers together and saying, "Tigers, Tigers, together we fight. Tigers, Tigers, in the night," which I thought was a silly thing to say. Then Harry said we were supposed to spit on the ground. I didn't like spitting and especially on Mum's shiny wooden floor. When we had all spat and Harry had rubbed it into the floor with his shoe Roger got some of Mum's lipstick and put red lines on our foreheads. It felt fantastic. I was one of their gang!

Roger told me to put the sandwiches and drink cartons in his rucksack and as I was a newcomer to The Tigers, I had to learn the rules. I asked him what the rules were but all he said was that he was the leader and Harry was second in command. He said I was a new initiate, but I wasn't sure what that meant.

We shouted, "we're off to the beach Mum," up the stairs and

Harry said, "Goodbye Mrs Elliot," but Mum must have been busy with Karen as we did not hear her reply.

It only took us about five minutes to get to the beach. The sand around the dunes is very soft but you have to be careful, Mum said, because the sand moves all the time and it has covered up the fences that used to stop the sheep getting on the beach. There are places you can just see the tips of the fences. We went further down the beach to where the dunes were the highest. Harry and Roger found some old fence posts and had a pretend sword fight. I went onto the hard sand and looked for shells and pretty stones. I found quite a few and put them in Roger's rucksack.

I got a bit bored looking for shells, there weren't many anyway, most of them were down by the water's edge and the tide was out a long way. I trudged up one of the dunes looking for Harry and Roger and found them laying down sunbathing.

"Can I have a sword fight with you Roger?" I asked.

"No, girls don't have sword fights. Girls have to wait to be rescued by their Knight in Shining Armour-or at least that's what happens on the tv." Roger said.

I protested and insisted someone sword fight with me. I picked up Roger's pretend sword and pointed it at Harry.

"Harry, come on. Please have a sword fight with me." I pleaded.

"Oh, all right then. Just this once." Harry stood up, legs apart and pointed his fence post at me. Harry bashed my stick and I bashed his and then I fell over and landed on a sharp piece of fencing that was buried in the sand.

When I got up bright red blood was gushing from my knee. I began to cry. Roger stood up, ran over and told me to stop crying and he and Harry would get me back home as quickly as possible. It was hard hobbling among the sand dunes. Harry held my left arm and Roger my right, but it was still quite difficult, and the rucksack was now rather heavy as It was full of pebbles and shells. We had not had any time to enjoy our sandwiches.

With a struggle Harry and Roger got me home although I left a trail of blood in the sand.

"Mum, Mum, Tracey's cut her knee open." Roger shouted as he opened the back door. I sat on the step grimacing because of the pain.

"What on earth happened Tracey?" Mum asked as she went to the cupboard and got out a bottle of disinfectant, the sort that stings when you put it on, some cotton wool and a packet of plasters.

"An Alligator bit me Mum. I was playing in the swamps with Roger and Harry and this Alligator jumped out from behind a fallen tree and it bit me right on the knee."

"Well it's a good job it was a small Alligator, or it would have gobbled you right up."

"Yes Mum, I said.

Roger and Harry glanced at each other, shrugged their shoulders, took the rucksack and sat at the kitchen table eating their sandwiches.

"How's Karen Mum?" I asked.

"Well she's only a tiny bit better. I'm sorry but you'll have to play with Roger and Harry for a couple more days now."

"I don't mind that Mum." I said.

21

KEVIN

"Can you keep a secret?" My sister Sarah asked as she stuck her head around my bedroom door. I looked up from trying to concentrate on my school homework and replied, "Of course, I can," while thinking, I know *you* can't, or you wouldn't be telling me now. "What's it about this time? Sarah was always confiding her and anyone else's secrets in me and then she'd generally spread them all over Facebook, while telling me not to tell anyone!

"It's about Mum."

"What about Mum?"

"I think she's having an affair."

"Don't be daft. What on earth makes you think that?"

"I heard her on her phone the other day. She was talking to Val, her friend who works in the corner shop. I heard her tell Val she couldn't wait to see Kevin."

"Well who on earth is Kevin? I don't know anyone around here with that name. I've never heard Mum speak of any Kevin before either."

"Shall we tell Dad Linda?"

"For goodness sake no Sarah. That's the last thing we want to do."

"Well what can we do about it then? I mean, if Dad should ever find out I don't know what might happen."

"We've got to discover the truth Sarah. You said you heard her mentioning Kevin on her phone. We need to know who this Kevin is. Investigate it first and then we can think of what to do next."

"How can we investigate it?" Asked Sarah.

I thought hard and then told Sarah my idea. "We can try and get hold of Mum's phone and look at the texts and numbers and maybe can find out exactly who he is."

"But Mum keeps her phone locked and I don't know the pass code. Do you Linda?"

"No, I don't." I had to think again. Plan B. "Sarah, one of us could distract Mum quickly while she's using her phone. Then we can grab it and go through the messages and numbers."

"But who's going to do what Linda?"

"I know, we'll wait until she's talking on her phone, then I'll come running down with my homework and say I can't do it and get all panicky and stuff so that she helps me. You're very quick on your mobile, so you can get Mum's phone and go through her numbers and texts while she's distracted. Does that sound a good idea?"

"That's great. We'll just have to wait for the best moment."

.....

Two days later I heard Mum talking on her phone to someone. She was in the kitchen. I sneaked into Sarah's bedroom and told her to hurry up as the game was on. Then I tiptoed back into my bedroom grabbed my homework and we both ran downstairs.

I crept behind Mum and then said, in a loud voice, "Mum,

Mum, can you help me please? I can't do my homework and it's got to be in by tomorrow."

Mum was not happy at being interrupted. "Can't you see I'm on my phone. I'm busy. Won't it wait Linda?"

"No Mum. I've got to hand it in tomorrow morning." I gigged about on my toes and tried very hard to make a nuisance of myself.

"Oh, come on then. I'll speak with you later, Val." Mum said and then grabbed my homework book. "What can't you do?"

"It's maths Mum. I don't understand algebra."

"Well you know I'm no good at maths and algebra either. You'll have to wait until your Dad gets home." She pushed the book back into my face.

"Sarah! What are you doing with my phone?"

"I was just looking at the pretty picture you had on the front of Linda and me, that's all."

"Well you just keep your nose out of my business and my phone. I don't go looking in yours now do I?"

"No Mum but you know my pass code to get into my phone."

"Then change it my girl. That's all you have to do-change it."

"Yes Mum," Sarah sulked.

I followed Sarah back upstairs. We sank our sad bodies into my bed.

"Did you find anything Sarah?"

"No. I don't know the numbers on Mum's phone so I couldn't say if any were odd ones. There were no texts with the name Kevin on them."

I was perplexed. What were we to do now?

"What can we do now Sarah?" I asked.

"I guess we'll just have to wait for another opportunity. Maybe keep our eyes and ears open as well."

"We can check the mail." I said. "Let's make sure we are downstairs before Mum is when the postman comes."

"That's a fantastic idea, Linda." And embarrassingly Sarah gave me a huge hug.

.....

A week went by with nothing much happening, and I had almost forgotten about Kevin and Mum's affair when Sarah charged into my bedroom looking frantic.

"Linda, Linda. I've just heard Mum on her phone to Val again and she said she would meet her at the cinema next Friday night to see Kevin. I heard her loud and clear. She's going to meet Kevin! What can we do Linda, what can we do?" Tears were bubbling up in Sarah's eyes, so I cuddled her for a couple of minutes.

"It's all right Sis, we'll sort this out. Look, we'll follow Mum to the cinema. I expect she's going to the main one in town so that will be easy. We'll just have to be discreet."

"But what can we tell Dad?"

"I don't think Dad will be here for the next two weekends as he's got some conferences to go to. So, we'll be on our own. It's going to be all right Sarah. We'll find out all about this Kevin and Mum's affair as soon as we can."

.....

The Friday of the cinema visit arrived. Sarah came into my bedroom so that we could listen out for Mum getting ready in hers. We also hid our shoes and coats under my bed so that we could get them on quickly. Mum came into the bedroom and we both sat looking busy doing our homework. Mum said she would be off shortly, and we must behave and not stay up too late. Mum also said she would be late home as she would probably go for a little night cap with Val in the restaurant near the cinema. Sarah and I gave each other a knowing look. We both knew Mum would not be going to the restaurant with Valerie but with the dreaded Kevin. As soon as we heard the front door close, we put on our shoes and coat and headed downstairs and out the door. Mum was already at the bottom of the road. It was dark but we could see her meet up with Val as they stood by the lamppost on the corner of the street.

Sarah and I dodged in and out of people's driveways as we crept along behind Mum and Val. It was imperative we did not give ourselves away.

We turned the last corner and watched Mum and Val go into the cinema. Then we hurried over the road, made sure they were nowhere to be seen and went to buy our tickets. Luckily it was rated PG-13 and no-one questioned us about our age. Sarah is thirteen and I am fourteen but we both look much older than that.

We waited until a group of people were going in and we hid ourselves among them. Luckily, they all went to the back of the theatre. We had decided to sit as far to the rear as possible so that we could get a good view of Mum when she met Kevin.

We had a good vantage point of where Mum and Val were, and we settled down to watch the film. I was longing to buy some popcorn and Sarah kept saying she wanted a drink, but we just had to sit it out. We were on an important mission to save Mum and Dad's marriage.

The film began and both Sarah and I were mesmerised by it. We both cried and little and forgot all about Mum and Val. Then the lights went up and Mum and Val had disappeared.

We both rushed out the doors and kept ourselves hidden in the hordes of people exiting the building. Once outside the cinema again I saw Mum arm in arm with Val and they were heading for the restaurant Mum had told us about. I poked Sarah because she appeared to be falling asleep on her feet. She nodded when I pointed out Mum and Val.

"What shall we do?" Sarah asked.

"We'll have to follow them. Kevin is probably already waiting in the restaurant."

Once again, we crept along dodging in and out of shop doorways. We did not want to blow our cover. On seeing Mum and Val enter the restaurant we decided to cross over the road and stand behind a large oak tree so that we could get a good view of the interior. We were lucky in that Mum and Val were sitting at a table in the window. Our mouths began to water, and our tummies rumble as we watched them order starter and then mains. Kevin was nowhere to be seen.

We were both feeling rather cold, disappointed and hungry now and so we decided to go home.

"I'm going to confront Mum in the morning." Sarah said as she stomped along beside me.

"I'm not sure if that's a good idea, Sarah. I think we need to use different tack ticks."

.....

The following morning, I heard Mum downstairs in the kitchen and then Sarah's bedroom door open and close with a bang. I dived out of bed, put on my dressing gown and dashed to the kitchen. There was Sarah with her hands on her hips.

"Mum, are you having an affair?"

"What a silly question child. Of course not. Whatever gives you that idea?"

"Kevin."

"Kevin?"

"I overheard you loads of times telling Val you were going to see Kevin. You went out with him last night, didn't you?"

"Well you cheeky little suspicious blighter, I went to see the film Dances With Wolves-STARRING KEVIN COSTNER! Do you really think I would betray your Dad? Is that what you think of me?"

Sarah was blushing. I watched as she rushed toward Mum and hugged her. "Sorry Mum. I was so worried when you kept mentioning Kevin and I didn't want you and Dad to split up."

"Kevin Costner-he's my favourite actor. That's all I went to see. Come on girls let me get you a nice breakfast. What say we have a good old fry up and no more talk of affairs please."

Luckily Mum saw the funny side and I did too. I also felt a great relief. We didn't dare tell Mum we had been at the cinema. It was a fantastic film and now Kevin Costner is also our favourite actor.

22

GRANDAD'S NEW TOY

"Hello, is that you Adam?"

"Yes Granddad. What's up?"

"Nothing my boy. Nothing at all. It's just that I've, gone and bought myself a computer."

"Hey, Granddad, well done. So, you've caught up with the times at last?"

"Now don't be cheeky lad?"

"Just joking Granddad. How's it going?"

"It's not. That's what I'm phoning you about. I need some help here."

"What do you mean it's not going Granddad?"

"I mean the screen, if that's what you call it, is completely blank. I've plugged it in at the mains, but nothing's happening. Just a black screen."

"You have to switch it on Granddad. It doesn't come on automatically."

"But I can't find a switch. That's why I thought it was broken. There's no switch, nothing, just this screen."

BARBARA BURGESS

Arthur heard the faint sounds of chuckling echoing down his mobile phone. "Either you run your hand along the front, near the corners or you put your hand around the back and find a button. It won't be very noticeable. You'll have to search for it."

"Oh, all right then, I'll try that. Wait a minute."

Arthur ran his hand along the front of his new computer. Nothing happened. With a sigh he felt around the back and discovered a small indentation into which he placed his fingertip.

"Ah, you've started it up then Granddad. I can hear the sound."

"Yes, thanks Adam. It seems to be working now. I've got a pretty picture of the seaside in front of me."

"That will be your desktop Granddad."

"My desktop? Why on earth is it called my desktop when I've already got a desktop? My computer is on my desktop and now I have another one. This is so confusing Adam."

Arthur smiled to himself as he shook his head.

"Hang on a minute Adam there's a rectangular box and a little line that keeps coming and going."

"It's called 'flashing' Granddad. The line is flashing to indicate something needs to be done. It wants your password. Have you got your mouse?"

"Mouse? Mouse? I'm not like you Adam with all your reptiles and that little tortoise you have. I kept mice and rats when I was your age, but I don't have any mice now, son."

"I don't mean a real mouse Granddad. I mean the thing you work the computer with. It's called a mouse. Did they give you a keyboard and another small device? That small device is your mouse."

"Yes, I've got what you call a keyboard with all the letters of the alphabet on it. It's not at all helpful though the letters are all over the place and not in alphabetical order."

"They're meant to be like that Granddad. It's like a typewriter keyboard."

"Oh, I never learned to type. Your Nan did though, and she was good at it. I will have to find the keys one at a time. It will take me a while, but I expect I'll get used to it."

"You need to hold your mouse Grandad and then you will see a little arrow come up on the screen."

"That's amazing Adam. Now what do I do?"

"Now you point your mouse, the arrow, at that flashing line and start typing in your password."

"But I haven't got a password. They didn't give me one."

"Did they give you a receipt Granddad?"

"Yes Adam, but I don't know where it is at the moment. I hope I haven't thrown it away."

"I expect they've put your password on the receipt for you. You'll need to find it."

"Well the very nice lady in the shop told me the computer was all set up and ready to go and I didn't need to do anything. I paid extra money for that. I'll see if I can find the receipt. I'll phone you back in about ten minutes Adam."

Arthur rummaged around in the drawers of his desk but failed to find a receipt. Then he noticed a piece of paper sticking out from a book sitting on a chair near him.

"There you are you silly receipt. Trying to hide from me. Now let's see if there's this password Adam wants. Ah, yes, there it is PASSWORD – plokij123."

"Is that you Adam? I've got the password. It's a bit weird it's plokij123."

"Type it in then Granddad. Then click the return key and it will open up your computer."

Arthur typed in the password and waited.

"What do you mean-return key Adam?"

"On your keyboard, there's a key on the right with an arrow that turns back on itself-like it's got a hook on it. Tap that."

"I think that's done it Adam. I think it's working now."

"Great Granddad. I'll leave you to it then."

"No, Adam. I don't know what to do next."

"What do you want to do then Granddad?"

"I don't know Adam. What can I do?"

"You can send me an email if you like. Just to get used to it and to see how it all works."

"Is that a bit like texting on the phone Adam?"

"Yes, it's a little bit like texting and you know how to do that don't you?"

"Of course, I do son. I'm not that daft."

"Right, Granddad. Open a window."

"I'm not opening any window. It's freezing out and it's just started snowing."

"I don't mean open a window Granddad. I mean open a window. Get your mouse and point the arrow at the little cross right at the top. This will open what we call a window."

"Oh, all these new words. I thought having a computer was going to be easy."

"It will be Granddad once you get used to using it."

"I hope so my boy. I really hope so. Now I've got this, what-you-call-it window thingy open so now what do I do?"

"Can you type in Hotmail Granddad and then click the return key again."

"h-o-t-m-a-i-l. Return key. I'm getting good at this. Done it Adam."

"Now Granddad I hope the shop has already signed you up to this. Or else you will need another password."

"Yes Adam, it looks as if it is working. The assistant did spend ages with me in the shop, but it was beyond my understanding. I wasn't going to let her know I'm a computer imbecile. I just went along with it. I pretended I knew what she was doing."

"Oh, Granddad, I'm sure they have many complete beginners go into their shop to buy computers. It's nothing to be embarrassed about."

"It's okay for you Adam. You were brought up with all this technology. You know how difficult it was for me to learn how to use that iPhone you helped me buy. This is even worse!"

"You'll soon get the hang of it Granddad. No need to worry. Now have you managed to get into your Hotmail account while we've been talking?"

"Yes. It all looks good."

"That's great Granddad. Now you can type me an email."

"Right, Adam. What shall I put?"

"Anything Granddad it doesn't matter. It's just to get you used to using the keyboard and mouse and becoming computer literate."

"Right, well here goes. h-e-l-l-o-a-d-a-m. I've typed it out so now what do I do?"

"You need to click your mouse on 'send'."

"Don't click 'delete' Grandad."

"Ooops."

23

NAN TO THE RESCUE

*M*um has a habit of booking holidays without anyone else knowing. She said it was a long time since we'd all spent a week together including Nan. A cottage on the Norfolk Broads was her choice this time. It has eight bedrooms, she said, so we could all be there and share.

I hate sharing. I loathe crowds. When our whole family is together it becomes a mob. Auntie Jessica often refers to us as 'the mob' when she talks to Dad on the phone. I also resent Nan being invited along.

Our family is huge. Dad has four kids from his first marriage- three boys and a girl. Mum has four kids from her first marriage- four girls. Three of these girls have also had girls. Then there's me and Charlotte who belong to Mum and Dad and if you add Nan then I've lost count.

As soon as Dad learned of the holiday, he started moaning about having to hire a minibus. He said he'd try and get as many of us in it as he could. The others, he said, would have to make their own way there. He also mentioned to blame Mum for booking it without consulting anyone.

Nan was invited to stay at our house the day before so that she could come in the minibus with us all. That meant Mum had to shuffle all the beds around the night before we were meant to be going on this fantastic holiday. That's what Mum called it anyway. I was sure the whole thing was going to be a disaster.

Sitting in any vehicle while Dad's driving is just a pain in the backside. He complains all the time about, "that idiot up my arse," or "that twit in front who's on a go slow." He'll shout about cars cutting him up or jumping in front of him at roundabouts. Then he'll say people with dogs on long leads are a menace to drivers. He goes on and on for the whole journey. I end up with a headache.

Nan, who insists on sitting in the front tells Dad whenever there are traffic lights. She instructs him when to brake. She sighs when he slows down and asks if we will ever get there. Then when Dad gets on the motorway she hangs onto her seatbelt for dear life and tells him he's going too fast. It happens every holiday and this one will be no different I'm sure of it.

The day of our holiday arrived. We reached the cottage with fewer mishaps than usual. That was a relief. Everyone made a mad scramble to nail a bedroom and make it their own. I refused to share with Nan outright. I'd done it before and never again. Nan snores and wanders around naked most of the time.

Mum suggested the three Great Granddaughters share one of the double beds in Nan's room. This cheered Nan up no end. The three little girls didn't seem to mind either. They thought it would be fun. I helped carry Nan's bag to her room and left the three girls using the bed as a trampoline. I laughed and wondered what they would get up to during the night. But whenever I'd shared with Nan, I found nothing woke her except the sun entering the room in the morning.

After we'd all unpacked Damien yelled that we should go to the pub for a meal. Miriam asked who was paying. Nan immediately said she shouldn't be expected to pay as she'd bought the petrol for the journey. Dad refused as he said he would probably end up paying for the whole holiday anyway on his credit card. He reminded everyone how Mum had booked it without his permission. Mum opened a bottle of wine and switched on the tv.

At six o'clock we all marched to the local pub. It was only ten minutes from the cottage. I discovered they do all day breakfasts there-my favourite.

Dad said it was 'each man for himself' as far as paying for the meal was concerned. But I did notice he paid for Nan's fish and chips. She somehow managed to get tomato ketchup all down her dress and Dad wouldn't stop tutting at her.

The following day Dad proposed we hire a canal boat. Mum thought there wouldn't be room for everyone on it. Then Nan suggested we leave her out. But Dad insisted she be included. So, we all got on a canal boat. The owner advised us all to put on our lifejackets or he wouldn't give Dad the key to the ignition. There were complaints all round, but we all complied in the end. The boat man then confessed that by law we should be sharing two barges with such a large family. He admitted he only had the one available so would oversee this error this time.

I wanted to steer it, but Dad wouldn't let me. He said It was too dangerous. It took us all day to go about half a mile and back, but it was fun. Nan and the three little girls loved throwing bread for the ducks. I enjoyed sitting on the roof. I watched the world go by, waved at the people on the tow path and the boats that went by.

Most evenings were spent trying to sort out the tv. Dad couldn't get it to work properly. He said it was due to where we were staying. The sound was too low-or maybe it was because Nan was snoring loudly again. Whenever Dad switched channels Nan woke up and said that was her special programme and not to change the channel. We had to watch whatever she liked. I hated all her programmes. They were boring and I got annoyed. Then Dad said Nan was our guest and she could watch what she wanted.

In the middle of our holiday everyone decided to go their own way for some reason. Maybe they were all getting fed up with being around each other.

Dad's other kids went off to visit some castle or other and Mum's other kids, who I didn't get on with that much, went off shopping. We were all left behind with the three little girls.

Dad decided we should go to the beach. I thought it a great idea and dreaming of ice creams and chips made my mouth water.

Nan kept saying she'd rather stay at the cottage, but Mum and Dad insisted she come with us as she would enjoy it. We hadn't been to an actual beach for several years now.

I was the first out of the car followed by Charlotte and the three little girls and we all ran to the sea. The tide was a long way out, but we got there in the end. The water was freezing.

Dad said we had to be careful as the tide can come in very quickly in Norfolk. He spent ages on his mobile phone trying to find out when high and low tide was.

Nan told him it didn't matter as we would all be safe anyway. We found some beautiful soft, dry sand up near the dunes and spread our blankets out.

Nan fell asleep immediately and began snoring again. Dad put up the wind shield. Mum poured out three glasses of wine and gave us kids orange juice and a cake. Dad then pumped up the Lilo.

Charlotte and I were busy building sandcastles with two of the little girls. Mum and Dad had joined Nan and were fast asleep. I didn't realise the tide was coming in. I didn't notice Kate, the smallest of Nan's Great Grandchildren sitting on the Lilo. Neither did I see it float out on the tide.

Charlotte was the first to realise that Kate was missing. She screamed, "Where's Kate?" It made me jump. The other two girls began to cry. Mum, Dad and Nan sat bolt upright and began searching.

Nan pointed and bellowed, "There she is. She's in the sea."

Well, I have never seen Nan run so fast in all my life. She was like a bullet from a shotgun. Off down the beach in her bare feet calling for help. She went straight into the water fully dressed and with the assistance of two strangers she dragged Kate and the Lilo back to shore.

It was all over and done with before Mum and Dad had even got near the edge of the water. Mum was crying. Dad was telling everyone off for not looking after Kate. Nan picked Kate up and gave her a kiss and cuddle and they were the only ones smiling.

Dad thanked the two people who helped Nan. Then he said we'd better get back to the cottage as quickly as possible so t

I was so proud of my Nan that day and have been ever since. I asked if I could share with her for the rest of the holiday. The three little girls were still in shock and so they wanted to sleep with their parents. Nan said I could. I said, "that's great Nan." And gave her a huge hug.

I was quite sad when the holiday was over. I asked Mum if we could book another one soon and invite Nan to come along. Mum said "yes-but don't tell your Dad yet."

"Let us always meet each other with smile, for the smile is the beginning of love."
    ~ Mother Teresa

24

WHAT NOT TO DO WITH OLIVE OIL

I can't tell you how many times someone has asked me about the scars on my skin. The blobs, patches and discolouration.

I don't mind telling them because I really haven't got a clue as to why I did it to myself. Yes, I admit it was my fault and I should have had more sense, but at the time, for some reason, I didn't.

I'd been listening to mum and dad talking about their holidays with nan and granddad. Their childhood and the things they did that people don't do any more.

They used to spend a week at the same B & B each year at Bognor. They'd have their breakfast and then go and find a nice spot on the beach where they could sunbathe for the rest of the day.

I always wondered why everyone but me had a lovely tan. I'm not a sun worshiper-they are. They must have got their original tan and then topped it up each holiday-plus the weekends in the garden.

They've all got different skin to me. Mum says I take after her side of the family, only way back. Great Grandma or someone further back in the family tree. My skin is fair, and my hair blonde. Mum's is darkish, although she said she was blonde when she was a baby. Dad's hair is a bit sort of blondey-ginger. Dad says it's 'girly hair'. He says men's hair should be dark brown or black. Nan and granddad on dad's side of the family are the same. Darkish hair and they tan easily.

I was listening to mum and dad and they were talking about how they used to put olive oil on their skin and then lay in the sun on the beach. They'd put the oil on their front and lay all morning and then turn over and do the same in the afternoon.

Mum and dad were laughing at how red they were at the beginning of the week but nice and brown by the end of their holiday.

I decided I was fed up with my fair skin and wanted a tan. I was also into boyfriends and there was this boy, James, I fancied. I was sure he'd like me more if I had a suntan. Mum also said the sun lightened her hair. So, I pictured myself with a super tanned catwalk body and light blonde hair snogging James.

Mum and dad said they were going out for the day and asked me if I wanted to go with them. Sight-seeing around a castle and ending up at a pub didn't appeal to me. I told mum I had my course work to catch up on and they left me behind. It was during the heatwave, early July.

I took the opportunity to try out mum's tanning technique.

There was a bottle of olive oil in the kitchen cupboard. I grabbed a towel, the oil and went out into the garden.

After spreading the towel on the concrete patio-yes it was a bit hard, but I thought the heat from the concrete might even tan my back. Where I got that idea from, I don't know!

I sat down and lathered myself with the olive oil. All over my front. My face. Some of it went in my hair. My body. Trying not to mess up my bikini. My legs. Everywhere. Then I lay down. I was planning on allowing about thirty minutes and then turning over. What happened was, I fell asleep for four hours! Yes, four hours in the blazing hot sun during a heatwave with oil on my body!

It was the neighbour's dog barking that woke me up. I looked at my legs and they still appeared white to me. I felt hot though. When I stood up, I came over all dizzy. I went inside, got one of dad's pint glasses, filled it with water and drank it. I thought I might be dehydrated. That made me feel much better.

Then, what on earth to do with all this oil, I thought. So, I ran myself a bath. Mum had been given some special bubbles from nan the week before for her birthday. I thought I could have a soak and enjoy the beautiful perfume and the oil would come off. It didn't-at least not much. It left a grimy mess around the side of the bath. I wondered how on earth I was going to clean it off. I didn't want mum having a go at me.

After about ten minutes soaking, I began to feel a bit wheezy. I thought again that I might be dehydrated but wanted to relax for a little longer. The water was becoming cooler. I needed to top it up. When I reached for the hot tap, I noticed my hands were bright red and looked a bit puffy. I then stuck a leg up and that too appeared very red and swollen and I was certain there were blisters bubbling up on it.

I was horrified and quickly stood up in the bath to examine the rest of me. It was then I nearly fainted. I felt extremely wobbly. My skin was burning. I could hardly breathe. I began to panic. I quickly pulled the plug out of the bath and put a towel around myself. The towel began to sting me as it touched my skin. Blisters appeared everywhere. I was distraught. What could I do? I daren't phone mum and dad as they would give me a right old rollocking.

I thought of calling my friend Angela but by this time I was feeling very faint so instead I dialled 999.

The paramedics were marvellous. They put an oxygen mask on me straight away. At the hospital the doctor asked me what sun block I'd been using, and I said olive oil. I could see by his face it was the wrong answer.

The doctor then asked how long I'd been in the sun and I said at least four hours.

He then told me I'd been like a big, fat sausage frying in olive oil for four hours and it's a wonder I wasn't all black and shrivelled.

I didn't much care for him insinuating I looked like a big fat sausage.

I was given an injection for the pain. Another one for my allergic reaction to mum's bubble bath. Another injection in case of infection and so it went on.

They put gallons of white cream all over me which was very soothing and told me to keep still. That was the hardest part. Keeping still, especially trying to sleep on my back all night long. I like to sleep on my tummy. That was out of the question for many weeks.

Someone must have told mum and dad that I was in hospital and they visited me. Mum kept crying. Dad kissed me on top of my head. They both wanted to give me a hug, but I think the white cream put them off a bit. I felt sore and fragile for at least two weeks after that.

I will say mum and dad were good to me. They didn't reprimand me they kept saying they were glad I was alright. They said it was clever of me to think of dialling 999.

Not long after I got out of hospital, I met James when I was walking past the local park. He was the first to ask me what on earth I'd done to my skin. We've been out together four times so far and he kissed me.

25

MISSING, PRESUMED DEAD

"Jack? Is it you? Is it really you? We thought you were dead!"

"It's me alright Lisa. Alive and well, though sometimes I think I'd be better off dead."

"You can't say that Jack. Here let me take a look at you."

Lisa placed her hands-on Jack's shoulders and looked him up and down.

"You've lost a great deal of weight, for sure. Where on earth have you been these past five years? Why have you suddenly turned up in town? We had a funeral for you. Missing, presumed dead, they said. We had a ceremony."

"I know, Lisa"

"You know? How? If you knew then why the hell didn't you tell us, you were alive?"

"I couldn't."

"What do you mean, you couldn't?"

"Look, can we go somewhere and talk? Somewhere quiet.

The café around the corner is often empty this time of day. I've been going there for my meals sometimes."

"What do you mean-your meals? I don't understand Jack."

"Let's go there anyway. We can talk. I can tell you what's been happening to me."

"I think an explanation might be a good idea Jack. After all your mum and friends deserve to know where you've been all this time. I'm getting angry here Jack. After nearly five years you turn up without any explanation. I don't think you're being fair on yourself or anyone for that matter."

Jack and Lisa turned left and headed for the pint-sized café. Three sets of tables and chairs stood neatly in a row outside. Inside the place was empty. Just one person behind the counter ready to take their order.

"Here, Lisa, let's sit in the corner. What would you like?"

"I'll get it Jack. You look as if you're skint."

"Thanks Lisa. I was hoping you wouldn't notice."

"It's obvious Jack. You're down on your luck good and proper. What will you have? I'm telling you a brandy wouldn't go amiss here; however, I'll stick to coffee and a flapjack."

"I'll have whatever you're having Lisa."

Lisa placed the order, then sat at the little round table opposite Jack. Resting her chin in her hands her eyes scanned the person she believed to be dead.

Long, greasy hair. A jawline covered in mottled stubble. Clothes two sizes too big even for his tall frame and broad shoulders. He looked nothing like the suited Jack she remembered from her post high school days.

Jack dived into the coffee and flapjacks as soon as they arrived.

"Slow down Jack. Would you like me to order a breakfast or some sandwiches?"

"No, I'm fine. I just love coffee and flapjacks, that's all. Sorry, I've lost my manners."

"So, Jack are you going to tell me what's been happening these past five years? Why you've been missing without trace or presumed dead?"

"Too many questions Lisa. Give me a chance."

"Sorry Jack. You don't know what it's been like for all of us here. Not knowing what's happened to you. We were told nothing. Everyone's been extremely worried and upset. Your mum has aged so over the past five years. She's just not herself. Why couldn't you at least have let her know you were alive?"

"I couldn't Lisa and that's that. So much has happened to me. I've been through hell and that's an understatement."

"All your mum got was a letter saying you were missing presumed dead. She had some visits from two weird men in grey suits who told her not to worry. That's all they said. Your mum was distraught, and they said they hoped she wasn't too upset."

"I'm sorry Lisa, but it had nothing to do with me."

"What do you mean it had nothing to do with you? I'm sure you could have visited your mum or phoned her at some point over the past five years. And what about Rona?"

"What about Rona?"

"Well, I will tell you Jack Sheldon, Rona has found someone else. Yes, and she's very happy too. They've just had a baby boy. They've called him Nicholas. They were going to name him Jack but then decided it would be Nicholas after your dad instead."

"Well, I'm glad Rona's made a fresh start. Honest I am. I hope they're happy together."

"Oh, they are Jack-and it's no thanks to you."

"Look, Lisa, I couldn't help the ship exploding and sinking, could I now? Everything went tits up after that. My life changed beyond words."

"Yes, Jack, we heard about the explosion on the news. Your mum was in total despair. Then we didn't hear anything. Not a bloody thing. You'd think the Home Office would have contacted relatives. No news or information about you for ages."

Jack squeezed Lisa's hand, trying to give her reassurance.

"Yes, the ship went down. There were six of us survivors. We floated for days. I really don't remember much. I was delirious most of the time with burns to my back. They told me we'd somehow climbed onto debris from the ship and floated along and landed on some island or other. The inhabitants found us all and we were then rushed to the local hospital. From there I was flown to Australia."

"Australia? Why Australia?"

"It was the nearest land mass to the island, and it had the best hospital facilities. Sydney."

"Sydney! So, you were in Sydney. How long for?"

"Four and a half years."

"Four and a half years, Jack! And you didn't think to contact anyone?"

"Look, Lisa. You don't understand."

"Too right I don't."

"I had burns to my back. My memory went. I couldn't recall a thing about the explosion and very little of what happened before or after that. I didn't know my name or rank either. It took me a long time to recover."

"Well I'm sorry to hear all that Jack but I do think you or the authorities should have told your mum. Given her hope."

"I know. It was all hush-hush. You know what it's like."

"No, I don't know what it's like Jack. I think it's all a load of bullshit to be quite honest."

"I had over ten operations on my back. Skin grafts taken from my arms and legs."

Jack pulled up his shirt sleeve to reveal the scars. Lisa recoiled in horror.

"If you think my arms look a mess then you should see my legs Lisa. I've had over forty skin grafts. My back's in a state too but I'm not going to show it to you here. I might get arrested. I've also had to learn to walk again and try and get my memory back. It's not been easy Lisa. I was asked if I wanted to contact anyone after they discovered who I was. I said no."

"You said no."

"Yes, I refused to let them tell anyone. How could I let people see me with all my injuries and hardly knowing who I was? It was a nightmare."

"Well you're here now Jack. So, what brings you to this place now of all times?"

"I'm trying to get my life back on track."

"Where are you living now?"

"High Beck."

"High Beck? That's a wood."

"Yes, High Beck Woods."

"You're living in High Beck Woods?"

"Yes."

"You're joking Jack. Tell me you're joking."

"No. I've been living rough ever since I got back to the UK. I can't face living in proper housing. They did give me a room, but it was so claustrophobic. I couldn't stand it. I have to be out in the open. I have to be aware of my surroundings. I have nightmares and palpitations and all that jazz that goes with the accident and memory loss."

"But where do you sleep Jack? What about washing and clean clothes and food and stuff?"

"There's a centre not far from here. I go there about once a month. They check me over, give me a shower, do my laundry and give me some food to take away if I need it."

"If you need it? What do you do for food the rest of the time then? Don't tell me you sit and beg. You're not a beggar are you Jack.? I can't stand this. My best friend from high school a homeless beggar."

"It's not like that Lisa. It's not like that at all. It's what I want. It's what I can put up with. I can't live in a house. I couldn't work if I tried. Noise just sends me off on one of my fits. I cannot bear to be with or near people at the moment. The doc' says it'll get better but so far it hasn't."

"Have you tried to get help Jack? Have you really tried?"

"Yes, Lisa. I get help all the time. Once a month from the centre. They're marvellous people in there. They don't put pressure on me. You're putting pressure on me right now Lisa."

"Sorry Jack, but it's been such a long time and as I said we were told you were dead."

"I know, but there's nothing I can do about that."

"We have a ceremony every year, at the church you know. The vicar is amazing to your mum. Very comforting. You've just got to see your mum and Rona. You'll have to forgive Rona, but she did her best after you disappeared."

"It's all such a mess Lisa. I really don't know what to do about anything, anymore."

"Look, Jack will it help if I come and see where you are living? Or would you like to come and live with Terry and me. We've got the space."

"No, thanks Lisa. I couldn't live with you and Terry. I told you living inside is not on right now. You can come to woods and look around. There are quite a few of us there. You can meet my mates."

Lisa finished her coffee.

"Tomorrow then. What time at the woods?"

"Noon will be alright with me and the other lads. Wait at the old stone bridge and I'll escort you to our little village. We call it The Village."

"Twelve noon tomorrow then Jack. Here let me give you a kiss. It's been such a long time."

Lisa kissed Jack on both cheeks and gave him a hug then left the café.

Early the following morning Lisa arrived at the stone bridge. Jack already waiting. They embraced. Lisa hung on a little longer, not understanding what was happening to her high school friend.

"Follow me Lisa. The path is quite narrow and a bit muddy in parts, but you'll be okay."

Lisa followed Jacks footsteps until they reached a small clearing that had a domed green tent in it.

"This is my home Lisa. Everything I own is either here or on my back."

"Well I must say it doesn't look as messy as some sites I've seen on the telly, Jack. I will say that. Can I look inside the tent?"

"Yeah sure."

"You haven't got many belongings. I can see your bedding and your cooking utensils and that's about it Jack. How on earth do you manage."

"Oh, I manage very well. We were taught survival as part of the job. There are so many ways you can survive, whether it's in the jungle or the desert. It's not that difficult when you know how. I enjoy looking after myself. I forage and we get stuff from the centre as well."

"Where are the other people."

"Oh, they preferred not to meet up today they said. So, it's just me."

"Well Jack, you can hardly invite your mum here and maybe not Rona either. What can I do to help you Jack? I want to help you reunite at least with your mum."

"No, no. Please leave Mum out of it. I really couldn't face her after all these years. I feel a bit of a fake and as I said my memory is not good. There's so much I can't recall. I might not even recognise her. You're lucky I noticed you in town yesterday."

"Oh, Jack but we've got to do something about you."

"Can you talk to the doctors at the centre next time you go. See if they can do something about your memory. Look, can we meet up again soon?"

"Yes, that will be great. I'll look forward to that. What about the same time next week at the café?"

"That's fine with me Jack. I look forward to it. Maybe you'll be able to tell me more of what has been happening to you."

"Maybe. Maybe not."

A week later Lisa arrived at the café as planned. Once again, she was early. She ordered two coffees.

At precisely twelve noon Jack's lank frame appeared in the doorway.

"You must have been here a while Lisa. I see you've already had two drinks."

"Yes, but I could do with another. I'll go and order them. Would you like some cake or a sandwich?"

"Cake will be great, thanks."

"I won't be a minute Jack; I need to powder my nose first."

"Okay. I'll still be here."

Lisa went over to the counter and ordered three coffees and three cakes and then went into the Ladies cloakroom.

"Are you ready Mary? Ready to meet your son Jack?"

"As ready as I'll ever be Lisa."

"Come on then. I'm right beside you."

Lisa took Mary by the arm and helped her back into the café.

Mary stood for a second frozen to the spot, her shaking body making Lisa feel anxious at what was going to happen.

"It's okay Mary, everything's going to be alright from now on."

With a soft, trembling voice Mary called out, "Jack."

Jack, startled, lifted his eyes from the table and looked across the café toward the lady's cloakroom.

"Mum?"

26

HERE COME THE SCONES

"Hi."

"Hello."

"Is this seat taken?"

"No."

"Mind if I sit on it? I much prefer the shade."

"Me too."

"Is this your first cruise?"

"Yes. Well no, really. I should be on another one."

"You're on the wrong cruise?"

"No. I'm definitely on the right cruise. I just chose not to go on the other one."

"Oh, where was that one going?"

"To Alaska."

"A bit different from the Caribbean then?"

"Yes. You could say that."

"I'd say a lot different. One place is hot and the other, I guess would be cold. Especially up on deck. No sunbathing like today."

"Yes, you're right."

"What made you choose this cruise then?"

"Oh. It's a long story and I'd rather not go into it here."

"No. I'm curious. Why on earth would someone change their mind about a cruise? Mind you, if I had the choice of hot or cold then I guess I'd still choose the hotter climate. Alaska can be beautiful, but I much prefer doing nothing all day long and sitting in the sun-or shade."

"Well, I might as well tell you. I've never met you before and I'm sure you won't spread it all around the ship. I'm here because of my mother."

"Your mother?"

"Yes, and my fiancé."

'Your fiancé?"

"Yes. I caught them snogging."

"You caught your mother and fiancé snogging?"

"Yes. The day of my wedding I caught my mum snogging my fiancé. In fact, they were more than snogging. He had his hand on her tits."

"Oh my god! That must have been awful. I mean a terrible shock. What did you do? Did you bash him one?"

"No. I carried on with the wedding and then left him."

"You carried on with the wedding and then left him?"

"Yes. I told him good riddance. I told him he could have my mother and I hoped they would live happily ever after."

"Well, I guess that might have been a brave thing to do. I'm not sure what I would have done under those circumstances. I think I might not have continued with the wedding. Yes, that's it. I think I would have run out of the church and left him forever."

"I wasn't in the church."

"Oh. Well wherever you were then."

"I was in the Limousine. We'd just stopped outside the church. We, that's me and my uncle. My uncle was giving me away, you see. My dad died of cancer last year. I wish he could have been there. He would have known what to do."

"Probably punch your fiancé in the face, I guess."

"No. Dad wasn't like that at all. Dad was always calm. He'd have given Gary a piece of his mind. I know that for sure. Anyway, if Dad had still been alive Mum would probably not have done it. She'd still be with Dad and not be feeling alone. She told me she felt lonely all the time."

"So, what happened next? When you arrived at the church in the Limousine?"

"I saw them. In the graveyard. They were actually near Dad's grave. I ask you. How could they do it, on Dad's grave? They were underneath the cherry tree. I know he had his hand on her boob and they looked as though they were loving it. Uncle saw it too. He told me to say nothing and to carry on with the wedding as everyone was here and everyone had spent a lot of money. So, I did. I just got on with it."

"You must have felt awful though. Taking your vows and that."

"Yes, I did. I felt as if I was in a daze. Dreaming or something like that. None of it felt real. I kept my eyes on Gary and then glancing over at Mum. Mum was giving me a questioning look all the time. She kept asking me if I felt okay. I said it was wedding nerves and that time of the month. That's what I told Gary that night. I told him unfortunately it was the wrong time of the month and he would have to go without. He stormed out of our hotel bedroom and came back in the morning."

"No! Do you think he went to your Mum's room?"

"I'm positive of that as they both appeared sheepish in the hotel dining room at breakfast. Gary hardly spoke to me and Mum kept on talking in a silly quiet voice."

"Well what did you do after that? I would have been livid. I would have thrown coffee all over Gary and slapped a cream cake in your Mum's face."

"No. I felt sorry for Mum. She looked drained. Pale and old somehow. I think nursing Dad had taken its toll on her. She was worn out. Her blue dress suited her, and she had a fantastic hat on, but she appeared weary."

"I like blue. If I was going to a wedding, then I'd wear blue. It's my favourite colour. I've been a bridesmaid twice-to my brother and my best friend. But I'm single at the moment and not looking for anyone either. I'm not on this cruise chasing a husband like some of these women."

"Me neither. Well I'm still married. But I'm not going looking for anybody-not yet, that is. I've had enough of men. Cheating men."

"So, what happened at breakfast then? Did you punch Gary? Did you confront him and your Mum?"

"No. Uncle joined us. He told me in the Limousine that it would all blow over. He told me to leave it and forget I'd seen it happen and it would all soon pass."

"Well I'm not sure if that was very good advice from your uncle. I mean, he probably meant well but not helpful advice at all. If it were me, I would have told the chauffer to turn the car around and take you back home until it was all sorted out with Gary and your Mum."

"Yes, with hindsight that is probably what I should have done."

"Too true."

"Well I did carry on with the wedding and the reception and the wedding breakfast the following day. Do you know what? We paid for over forty guests to stay at that hotel for four days. It cost us thousands. Or rather it cost Gary thousands. He paid for everything. Mum hasn't got any money. Dad didn't have a penny to his name when he died. No insurance-nothing. Mum hasn't got a clue what Dad did with his money. She thinks he gambled it away, but she hasn't got any proof. He did have some wins on the horses occasionally. He once won a thousand pounds because some football team lost. But he had no money at all. That's what Mum cannot understand. We all had to help her out with the funeral and everything. It was a very tough time for her."

"Your poor Mum."

"Yes, poor Mum except when she stole my fiancé. I had no idea what was going on. They could have been seeing each other for years, all the time I'd known Gary."

"Did you have any hints about their relationship?"

"No. Well, yes. I've been wracking my brains ever since. I thought of all the times Gary said he was busy or working late or couldn't see me. I tried to think of the dates. I tried to work out what Mum was doing at that time. There were a couple of weekends when me and Gary did not see each other, and Mum had gone away too. Mum asked me to look after Dad as she needed a break. I thought nothing of it at the time. But now, thinking back, I can see that the two of them were often out of my site at the same time."

"Oh, that must be awful for you."

"Yes, it was. Still is. I lay in bed at night trying to work out all those days and weekends when I looked after Dad and Mum went off somewhere. She wouldn't say where she was going. She said she was with a friend. I believed her. Silly me. I believed her. How stupid can a person get?"

"Oh, I'm sure you're not stupid. I expect this kind of thing happens to most people. I mean, a lot of people. I'm sure it's more common than you think."

"What? Your mum going off with your fiancé and snogging right before your eyes. I would think that is very rare. Hang on a minute my phone is ringing. It's Mum. She keeps on calling me and I refuse to answer. I'm thinking of blocking her soon."

"Don't you think you ought to answer her. Especially if she keeps on phoning. There may be something wrong. It might be an emergency."

"Yes, you could be right. I'll go back to my cabin and contact her. I've got my laptop with me. I can do a video call with her and see what's up. Make sure she's all right. I'm not going to forgive her though. She's made her bed and she can lie on it for all I care. Look can we meet back here and maybe order coffee and cream scones. In about an hour. That will be nice. Oh, by the way, I don't know your name."

"Maryanne. My name's Maryanne. And yours?"

"Felicity. Pleased to meet you Maryanne. Back here in about an hour then for coffee and scones."

"Yes. I'm not going anywhere. I've got my book and I might even have a little snooze."

***

"Mum. You keep phoning me. Is there something wrong? What's the matter? You needn't think I'm going to forgive you and Gary. No chance."

"No dear. I don't expect you to. That's not what I've been trying to ring you about. Are you enjoying your cruise? Gary managed to get some money back from the cancelled Alaskan cruise."

"Oh, did he. Well isn't that just lovely. He's got plenty of money anyway. He wouldn't miss a few thousands. I'm surprised he didn't take you with him Mum. A little honeymoon for both of you."

"Now there's no need to be sarcastic Felicity. I had a terrible time looking after your dad and I deserved some kind of comfort once in a while."

"Comfort! Comfort! Is that what you call it?"

"No, I don't mean that. Anyway, you'll never understand. Gary is so..."

"I don't want to hear another word about Gary, and I don't even want to hear his name ever again. I want to know why you keep ringing me Mum."

"Well I've found out where all your Dad's money went to Felicity."

"Where? Gambling? Horses?"

"No. Now I know it will be a bit of a shock for you."

"What do you mean Mum? Come on. Out with it. Let's get it over and done with. I'm sure one more shock won't hurt."

"Well your Dad had a lover, apparently."

"What?"

"Yes, and I'm as surprised as you are. She came to the house a few days after you'd gone on your cruise. She said she'd heard about you and Gary. Though I don't know where from. She came to apologise she said. But I was so taken aback and not sure I wanted to hear about any apology. She showed me photos of her and your dad, together. Apparently, they'd known each other for over ten years, and she's got a little boy."

"She's got a little boy?"

"Yes. Jamie. His name is Jamie. He's ten years old."

"I don't believe this Mum. Are you telling me Dad had a lover and has got a love child?"

"Yes, darling. I am. Your dad has had a lover for over ten years and has got a child called Jamie, by this woman. That's where all his money went. She showed me pictures of her home and garden. It's beautiful. Really big. Not like our tiny little bungalow where I nursed your dad all that time."

"Oh Mum. I don't know what to say."

"There's nothing you can say. At least we know he didn't gamble his money away after all."

"But we had to scrimp and scrape for his funeral and pay off all his debts. It's not fair, Mum. It's not fair on you or me."

"I know darling but it's something we've got to live with. Oh, by the way me and Gary are finished. I've met someone else. I met Fred at the bowling last week and we hit it off straight away. He's very nice and kind and gentle. We get along well together."

"I'm glad for you Mum. Look, we'll have to talk about all this when I get back. Enjoy spending time with Fred. I've just been talking to a very nice lady I've met. She's called Maryanne. I said I'd meet her on deck shortly for a coffee and some lovely cream scones. The food here is amazing Mum."

"Ah, glad you are enjoying yourself. Me and Fred are going to the cinema tonight."

"That's nice. Okay. Got to go now. Love you Mum."

"Love you too Felicity."

***

"Hi Maryanne."

"Hi Felicity. I've ordered the coffee and scones. It'll be here in about five minutes. Did you get to speak to your Mum?"

"Yes. She's okay. She's found out where dad spent all his money. Apparently, he had a lover for over ten years, and they've got a love child together."

"Oh my god!"

"Look, here come the scones."

27

APRIL FOOL'S DAY

What surprised Brenda the most was the dark blue of the door. Somehow, she was half expecting to see faded yellow and flaky paint. The piece of brown wood still nailed along the bottom. Someone had kicked a panel in one night. The two red steps where the colour tried desperately to peep through the grime now shone brightly.

Someone must clean and polish those steps every day, she thought, from her vantage point across the road. The brass doorknob appeared golden against the dark front door.

The sun always rose on this side of the house and warmed the step. She'd sat there many times trying to get her stiff body to move. A strange moment when she'd felt something akin to pleasure. Then Rosa shouting and asking who the bloody hell she thought she was sitting there like lady muck. She'd run back to the cold bedroom. Her bare feet not noticing the rough wood on the stairs. She'd curl up with the other kids on the filthy mattresses. Listening for the sound of Rosa leaving the building. Able to breathe again.

Brenda stood on the pavement opposite the terraced houses. Certain it was the door on the right and not the brown door on the left. She felt rather confused after all these years. It was the last house before the passageway that led to the rear yards. Yards with outside toilets where she'd sat for what seemed like hours. A means of escape. Not wanting to move or tear a sheet of newspaper from the hook in case someone heard the rustle and found her.

She remembered the spot opposite number thirteen. The place next to the lamppost where the dog always sat barking. She recalled his dry, dull coat. His protruding ribs. She didn't blame him for running away after a beating. She'd wished she could run away too, many times. Being so young, she hadn't known where to run. Where could she go? To the park? To the hills she saw through the mucky bedroom window. What about the other kids? Would they go with her? Would little Billy run away with her? She'd begged him once, but he hadn't answered, he just carried on crying.

Knowing he'd eventually find food probably brought the hungry dog back, Brenda thought. She understood what hunger felt like.

Rusty would run up the stairs to snuggle up with the friendly kids. He was a clever dog. Brenda watched him and learned from him. She learned how to steal food. Just enough for Rosa not to notice. That way no-one got a beating.

Brenda hung onto Miranda's arm.

"Are you okay, Brenda?"

"Yeah, sure. Let's just look at the old builder's yard for a minute, can we?"

"Yes, of course."

Brenda stared at the stack of bricks by the open gates. The old cement mixer. The mounds of wood and metal sheets. It all appeared just as she recalled it, apart from the piles being much larger. The building materials in the same place as if it were yesterday and not forty years later. A shiver crept up her spine.

"Are you sure you want to do this, Brenda?"

"Yes, I'm certain. Let's get it over and done with once and for all."

"I'll phone the estate agent. Their number's on the board. We can pretend we want to view the house. It's that or we just knock on the door and tell the owners you used to live here once. See if they will let you have a look around."

"No. I think I'd rather pretend to be a buyer if that's all right with you Miranda. I don't want people asking questions about how long ago I lived here and things like that."

"I understand. I'll give the estate agent a ring. I'll tell them we are only in the area for the day looking at properties. We need to view the house now as we've just come across it while looking in the area. Does that sound about right Brenda?"

Brenda nodded as she continued to scrutinise the builder's yard.

"Ah, is that Jackson's estate agents? We're standing outside a property. I got your number from the 'for sale' board. We wondered if we could view it, like now, as we are right outside, and it is in the area we are looking at."

Brenda heard muffled sounds coming from Miranda's phone.

"That will be lovely thank you."

"It's the smells."

"What?"

"It's the smells I remember the most."

"The smells?"

"Yes. The wood in the builder's yard and the dust. The sound of metal. I remember the sound of metal."

"Ah that's interesting Brenda. Maybe more memories will come back to you as we go around the house."

"I don't want memories coming back to me. I want to forget it all and put it in the past."

"No, of course you don't. I didn't really mean that."

"What did you mean then?"

"I don't know. Look, the estate agent says we can view. She will phone the owner and we can just knock on the door and she'll show us around. Are you ready for it?"

Brenda nodded, "Yes, I guess so. It's now or never."

Three minutes later, the front door of number thirteen opened. A smart-looking lady of about thirty-five stepped out onto the pavement and waved them over.

Brenda's legs went wobbly as she crossed the road, still hanging onto Miranda's arm.

"You're wanting to view, are you?"

"Yes please. We're only in this area for the day and this looks a lovely house and would suit us enormously. Thank you."

"Thank you," said Brenda.

The neat-looking lady led the way. Brenda put her right foot on the red step. Her mind shot back in time. Another smell. Little Billy had shit his pants as he'd run out the front door one day. The shit had dripped onto the step. No-one had ever bothered to clean it up. Instead, it had slowly dried in the morning sun. You just had to avoid it whenever someone took you in or out.

Miranda whispered, "Are you all right, Brenda? You look pale, my dear."

Brenda squeezed Miranda's arm to let her know she was fine.

They followed the owner down the narrow hallway. Brenda looked at her feet. She was standing on the same black-and-white tiles, now clean and nicely polished. Three cracked ones just inside the door. The walls a bright off-white. No bits of torn wallpaper dangling. No dirty marks. No spots of blood where little Billy had a nosebleed after being pushed down the stairs.

Little Billy was the only kid she could remember. Somehow, she recollected there being at least nine children at one time. Crammed into the middle bedroom. Filthy mattresses on the floor. Another shiver went through Brenda's thin frame.

"This is what we call the front room."

Brenda walked past the open white door and stared at the fireplace. Still there. The open grate now filled with fresh logs. Brenda took in the smell of the pine. A vase of roses sat on the mantle shelf. Beautiful pink roses reflected in the ornate mirror hanging on the chimney breast.

"We don't use the fire. It's just for decoration, really. Now we've got the central heating in. This place was so cold when we first bought it. All mod cons now. You'll love it. We do. But we've decided to move, and that's that."

Brenda relived the icy nights when all the children would huddle together to keep warm. If Rosa took pity on you and left a cloth to wash yourself with, then it would be frozen by morning. The sash windows never did close properly, and the wind whistled through the gap, keeping Brenda and some of the youngsters awake night after night.

"It's lovely," Said Brenda as she gazed at the clean white embossed wallpaper, the gloss paintwork, the picture of a sunset on the wall above the sofa.

Her mind flew back to the dimly lit room full of men with dirty yellow teeth. The smell of alcohol and cigarettes.

They would drag Billy downstairs first. When he came back up to the middle room, as they called it, Brenda knew it was her turn.

They passed her around the men. One at a time. They'd

cough in her face and laugh at her and force whisky down her throat until it stung.

Anger suddenly blew up inside Brenda. She tried to stifle it.

"Can we view the other rooms now please? You've got a lovely home here."

"Yes, this way to the kitchen."

Brenda recognised the step down into the room. The window on the right. The door to the yard at the far end. The scene forced up more memories. The damp smell. The old laundry pulley was still attached to the ceiling above the new-looking built-in oven.

Brenda's mind flashed back to the scene of Rosa standing at the cooker and Big Bob coming in from the yard and releasing the pulley onto Rosa's head. The washing catching fire. Big Bob getting some buckets of water and putting the fire out and then sending Rosa to the hospital to get her burns seen to. That was a terrible night. With Rosa away, more men came in. There were several kids in the front room with Brenda that night.

Rosa returned the following morning with her arms in bandages. Big Bob fixed the laundry pulley. Rosa hugged him for mending it.

"Would you like to see the yard?"

"No. I think that's okay. Thank you."

"We've turned the outside toilet and coal barn into a nice little shed. My husband keeps all his knickknacks in there."

"That's nice." Commented Miranda as she followed Brenda to the bottom of the stairs.

"I think I've seen enough." Brenda blurted.

"Are you sure?" Asked the lady of the house. "Maybe it's not what you were looking for after all."

"No. I mean, yes. I think it looks really lovely. The colours. The wallpaper. The fireplace and the kitchen. They all look very nice now. I mean, they all look very nice and warm and welcoming. Not a bit like what I was expecting."

"We've had a long journey to get here and we've got some more houses to view." Said Miranda as she edged her way back to the front door.

"That's all right. If you want to view again then do, please let me know. We are open to offers as the house has been on the market for a while and we are keen to move now we've set our hearts on it."

"We will. Thank you. We'll discuss it with the estate agents and they'll let you know. Thank you for showing us around."

"You're very welcome."

Brenda hurried out the front door and then hesitated on the top step. The smell of dog piss and Billy's dried up shit seemed forever stuck up her nose.

"Come on, Brenda. We'd better be off now. Brenda? Brenda? Are you all right love you've gone very pale?"

Brenda had her head down, looking at the pavement as she ambled along beside Miranda.

"I know my actual name isn't Brenda and I don't feel like a Brenda. I never have done since that day they found us all cooped up in that god-forsaken hole. They gave me that name. They didn't ask me if I wanted it. They just gave it to me when I said I didn't know what my name was."

Brenda started sobbing.

"I know. I was hoping you'd feel better for seeing the house again."

"Oh, I do. I do. They've made it look so lovely. I think they've loved that house. It's no longer got those horrors in it. Poor Billy. I wonder what became of him and the other kids?"

"Unfortunately, Brenda, it was impossible for us social

workers to give you and the other children access to names and addresses because of the court case."

"I know Miranda. I'm glad the house looks nice. Calm and peaceful somehow. Shall we go to that little tearoom we saw around the corner and celebrate my birthday now, Miranda? They may have given me a name I hate and 1st of April for my birthday, but we can still be happy."

"Yes, why not? It may be April Fool's Day, but you're definitely not a fool Brenda."

"Neither are you Miranda. Come on."

Brenda hurried along the narrow footpath to 'Betty's Tea Rooms' and ordered afternoon tea for two in the sunny garden at the rear.

"I remember very little about the night they raided the place Miranda. There was a lot of noise. I suppose they had to bash the door in. Then people everywhere. A lady took my hand and told me to follow her. They wrapped blankets around all the kids and stood them in the middle of the road to wait for the ambulances. I enjoyed having a warm shower and the soup."

Miranda gave a comforting squeeze to Brenda's arm.

"Here comes the splendid afternoon tea, Brenda. Just look at those neat sandwiches and the creamy scones, how wonderful."

Miranda poured two cups of tea. "Here Brenda, let's have a toast with our cuppa. Here's to…"

"April Fool's Day. My birthday." Brenda butted in.

"Yes, cheers. Happy Birthday and happy April Fool's Day, Brenda."

"Here's to a bright future for us both, Miranda."

28

THE PUDDLE DIPPERS

"Hi Dad, can you look after Arianne today for me? Work phoned. They want me to attend a conference as the boss has called in sick."

"Yes, no problem Vikki."

"Great Dad. I'll be there in about thirty minutes? See you shortly."

Vikki put the phone down, stood at the mirror, tidied her hair and checked her makeup.

"Are you ready, Arianne? Take your hiking boots with you. I'm sure Gran and Granddad will want to go for a walk in the woods."

"Okay Mum. Won't be long."

Ten minutes later eleven-year-old Arianne came skipping downstairs, her rucksack slung over one arm and the sleeve of her jacket dangling off the other arm.

"Here, let me help you." Vikki reached over to grab the back of the jacket and help to integrate arm and sleeve fully.

"I can do it, Mum. Stop fussing."

"Come on then. Let's get in the car or I'll be late."

"Why do you have to go in today Mum?"

"To be quite honest, Arianne, I haven't got a clue. The secretary could easily have gone in my place."

Arianne sat beside her mother, fastened her seat belt and took a book from her rucksack.

"What are you reading?"

"History homework, Mum. I've got to remember some dates and names of battles."

"Have a chat with Gran and Granddad, they love reading about history. I'm sure they'll help you."

"I will, Mum. It's not many dates, so I'm sure I'll remember them for Monday."

Twenty minutes later they reached the house on Seymour Street.

Vikki opened the car window and leaned out to kiss Arianne.

"Now be good and I'll phone you when I know what time I'll be back. If I'm going to be late, then you can stay over."

"Yippee." Arianne giggled, kissed her mum and ran up the steps to number seventy-seven. Gran and Granddad were waiting by the open front door. All three waved as Viki sped off down the road.

"Hi Gran and Granddad." Arianne gave her grandparents a kiss.

"Gran, can I stay over? Can you phone mum and tell her I'm staying over? I hope we can go for some long walks too."

Greg looked at Hannah, his eyebrows raised.

"Yes, you can stay over. I'll send your mum a text. She won't want to be disturbed while she's at the meeting."

"I'll take my bag up and put it on my bed."

"The *spare bed* Greg chuckled to himself." Hannah grinned. "Well, she certainly makes herself at home."

Two minutes later Arianne came galloping down the stairs. "Can we go for a walk in the woods? I love the woods, they are so magical."

Once more Greg and Hannah looked across at each other. *It's been raining a lot the last few days.* Greg mouthed to Hannah. Hannah shrugged her shoulders.

"Are you sure you want to go to the woods today? It's been raining and it will be muddy with lots of puddles."

"No Gran, that will be lovely. I love puddles. I've brought my waterproof hiking boots with me because I was hoping we could go for a long walk. Maybe take a picnic, too. What do you think, Granddad?"

Hannah sighed and beckoned Greg into the kitchen. "She wants a picnic too." Hannah chuckled.

"What's wrong with that?" Asked Granddad, confused lines spreading across his forehead.

"It's not the picnic I'm worried about, it's the puddles and the fact that she's twelve years old next weekend."

"Well, she can come and stay next weekend as well and maybe for some extra days."

"No, Greg, you don't understand. That's not what I'm getting at. The point is she's shortly to be twelve."

"Oh, twelve. I get it. But not till next weekend anyway, so we're probably all safe."

"I'm not so sure. She says she loves puddles. What if she decides to jump in one?"

"Oh, stop fussing. She'll be fine. I don't think she's ready. Besides, what she doesn't know about won't concern her."

"Well, I hope you're right, Greg."

Hannah placed six slices of bread onto the breadboard and buttered them. I think we'll have ham and cheese. She said absentmindedly. Once done she placed the sandwiches into individual polythene bags. Then put the little bags into Greg's rucksack along with a flask of hot coffee and a carton of orange juice for Arianne.

"Now Arianne, have you had some breakfast this morning?"

"Yes, Gran."

"Are you still hungry or shall we get off to the woods?"

"Can I have an apple to eat on the way?"

"Yes, of course you can." Hannah held out the bowl of dark red apples and Arianne took the large one sitting on the top of the others and bit into it.

"Um, juicy." She said as she wiped a drip off from her chin.

"Come on, Granddad. Are we going in the car to Beck Woods? I love the little stream there and the lake. I wonder if there will be any geese on it today."

"Yes, Arianne, if you insist, we can go to Beck Woods. However, I suspect that wood will be the dampest as it is on lower ground. The one up at the top of the village might be a better idea as that wood is on high ground and the land often drier."

"No Grandad, I choose Beck Woods. I don't mind a few pddles and some mud."

Once more Greg gave Hannah a worrying look. "Ah well, we can only hope for the best, Hannah."

The tiny car park at Beck Woods was completely empty apart from piles of rubbish.

"Look at this mess." Said Greg. "Why can't people take their litter home with them. Disgusting. Come on, everybody out. Bring the picnic with you. I don't really want to sit here and eat while looking at this lot. We can sit by the lake if there aren't too many flies."

"I'm Ready," said Arianne. "Can I take your bag Gran?"

"No dear, I think you've got enough to carry as it is."

"I've only got my book, and I grabbed another apple and mum gave me some biscuits. My rucksack is not that heavy."

Greg locked the car, checked the doors and placed the keys in his jacket pocket, keeping them secure by doing up the zip.

Arianne skipped ahead, admiring the various trees. Oak, Pine, Beech.

"Do you think we'll see any deer today Granddad?"

"Well, if you want to see some deer, you need to be quiet and walk slowly."

"Well, you know me Granddad, I don't know how to walk slowly. I just love the woods and the countryside so much."

Greg turned to Hannah, and they both smiled, pleased to be out with their only grandchild.

Greg looked at his watch. It was eleven thirty.

"Let's head up toward the lake. By the time we get there we'll be hungry, and we can have our picnic. Take that path to your left Arianne." Hannah shouted.

Arianne took the left path and ran her fingers along the top of the tall grass. She felt so excited it was as much as she could do to hold back and not run and run forever. A smile crossed her face, and it lit up in wonder at all the birds chirping. The puffy white clouds hovering in the rich, blue sky.

"Oh, look Granddad, there's a big puddle ahead. Can get around it somehow?"

Hannah turned her head quickly to look at Greg. Concern spread across her face.

"I knew this would happen."

"What do you mean?"

"You know what I mean. She's almost twelve."

"So what?"

"Well, you know what happened to me on my twelfth birthday. It's all right for you. You were born like it. I had to learn the hard way."

"The quick way." Greg corrected Hannah.

"Oh, all right then. The quick way. Still, it was a hard lesson to learn back then. I don't want that for Arianne. I want her introduction to be smooth. Come on, Greg, we've got to get to the puddle before she decides to fall in–or something even worse."

"Oh dam, look, my bootlace has come undone. You go ahead. I'll catch you up in a minute."

"Arianne," Called Hannah. "Wait. Granddad will be along in a minute. He's tying his bootlace. Wait and we'll find a different path around the puddle."

Hannah neared the puddle and could see how large and deep it was. It completely covered the path. The dark water reflected the trees above it. A mirror image of the sky, the clouds and the vegetation.

"Doesn't it look lovely, Gran? I always think puddles look as if you can go deep into them. One dive and you are in."

"No!" Exclaimed Hannah as she grabbed Arianne by the hand and began to shake.

"What's up, Gran? I didn't mean it literally."

Hannah made out to chuckle as she stifled her fear.

"Let's wait for Granddad. He knows this wood better than me, and he can guide us to a path to avoid all this water. We don't want to get our boots wet now, do we?"

"I don't mind Gran."

"Do hurry up, Greg."

"I'm trying. My lace has broken. I'm just fixing it. Won't be a minute."

Hannah sighed.

"Look Gran. Look into the puddle. Isn't it amazing? You can see the sky and the clouds and the....."

Arianne stepped up close to the puddle. The toe of her left boot touched the water. It rippled. Enormous waves of water began to roll back and forth. Hannah took hold of Arianne's elbow just as Greg leaned as far forward as he could and grabbed the back of Arianne's coat.

The group of three went deep, deep, deep, down into the puddle.

Arianne felt at one with the water. Neither hot nor cold, wet nor dry. She just was. She felt as if she were a silver, shimmering being from another planet. A sensation she had never experienced before.

Where was she? She asked herself. She knew she was no longer in the woods. She also knew that she had stepped on the edge of the puddle and watched the ripples turn into waves. Her sock had felt wet, even though her boots were supposed to be waterproof. She felt as if she were gliding and swimming at the same time. Just moving and being at one with the water. Then she realised she could breathe. She was under water and breathing.

She saw that a shimmering light and thousands of tiny air bubbles surrounded her. Her hands by her side, making her streamlined. She dare not look around, she just hoped Gran and Granddad were with her. She had felt them grab her but could no longer feel their hands on her clothing or her body.

The entry into the pond had been sudden. However, it seemed natural at the same time. The gliding appeared normal too. She was weightless. Then gently she landed and stood upright. She could now feel Gran's hand still on her elbow and Granddad's hand was not holding her coat anymore, instead it was holding onto a beautiful blue dress. Her hair had changed from dark to light and she thought she might be more like Alice in wonderland than Arianne Carpenter.

Arianne looked down. Her feet were bare. She was standing on soft golden sand. In front of her was a pool of the clearest, freshest water she could ever imagine. Fish swimming in it. They were congregating around the edge. Opening and closing their mouths as if they wanted to talk to her. She tiptoed over to them and placed her hand in the water. She could hardly feel the water. She could have sworn the fish were squeaking in high-pitched voices and saying hello in unison. She smiled and said hello back as she rippled the water with her fingers. The fish appeared to giggle and play with the ripples.

"Look Gran and Granddad. Look."

Hannah and Greg both smiled and gave a knowing nod to each other.

"Well, I'm relieved that went well." Greg held onto Hannah's arm.

Arianne swung around. "Where are we?"

"Well Arianne, I was hoping this wasn't going to happen to you quite yet."

"What do you mean Gran? I don't understand. One minute we were at the puddle and now we are here. What's happening?" A tiny tear left Arianne's eye.

"Don't fret Arianne." Greg put his arm around his granddaughter.

"The same thing happened to your Gran on her twelfth birthday."

"But I'm not twelve until next weekend."

"I know but obviously you are ready."

"Ready for what?"

"We are known as Puddle Dippers. Granddad has been able to dip into puddles and other worlds since the moment he was born. He'd go with his parents to the woods and they'd somehow lose him in a puddle and have to call the police. Actually, they had not lost him, he had just gone puddle dipping and his parents knew nothing of this at first. Then, after hours of the police searching the woods, they'd find him fast asleep by the side of a puddle. The police really thought there was some strange kidnapper in the woods who kept grabbing children and then bringing them back again and dumping them. Granddad thought it was so natural that he did not think he needed to explain what had happened. He thought he had fallen asleep at first and then he began to draw pictures of these other worlds and he began to write about them too. Eventually he was able to puddle dip at will and not just by accidentally getting too close to a puddle, the same as you did."

"But what about you, Gran?"

"Well, I learned exactly the same way that you did. I was out with your Great-grandparents and I tried to jump over a puddle and fell in, or rather fell through it and into this other world. When I came around luckily, your Granddad had been walking in the woods with his parents and saw what had happened and they helped me and explained everything to me. That's when I first met your Granddad."

"You've known Granddad since you were twelve? Wow."

Arianne looked around. "But we appear to be in a cave. Look at the entrance, Gran. The sky is so blue. Can we go outside and look around?"

"Of course. All you need to do is to think yourself there and you will be there. Come on, I'll show you how. Let's hold hands."

Hannah took hold of Arianne's left hand, and Greg held onto the right. "Ready–let's go outside the cave and look around."

Once more Arianne felt herself floating, gliding, streamlined. Her fine blue dress trailing around her ankles.

"This is fantastic, Gran."

Arianne's feet touched a hard, cold rock. She looked down.

"What's the matter Arianne?"

"I much prefer the warm sand and water inside the cave to this cold rock."

"Then change it."

"Change it?"

"Yes, you can change it with your thoughts. Just as we thought ourselves to the outside of the cave you can think anything you like and change anything you like."

"Can I change the rock to gold?"

"Of course. Just close your eyes and believe that you are standing on a rock of gold."

Arianne closed her eyes and screwed up her face. When she opened them, the rock had turned golden.

"Wow Gran. That is amazing."

"You can change anything you like by just thinking your thoughts."

"That's fantastic, Gran. Can I change the sky to pink?"

"Of course."

With that the sky became pink, and four deer appeared along with a squirrel. Arianne chuckled to herself.

"I could have so much fun here, Gran."

"I know darling, but we must get back and have our picnic before the sun goes down in the otherland."

"Is that what you call it—the woods—the otherland?"

"Yes, Granddad and I call this our magicland and the woods and where we live, we call—the otherland."

"But how do we get back?"

Greg came over and held Arianne's hand. "I'll show you. As you are new to this, I suggest we all hold hands again. Luckily, we could grab you just as you touched the puddle on your way in. Maybe if we hadn't, then you might not have made it quite so quickly. Now let's think of the lake where we want to have our picnic. Just keep thinking of the lake all the time and we'll be back there in a jiffy."

Arianne screwed up her face and thought as hard as she could. She pictured the lake with the geese on it and the grass around the edge and sky being reflected in it. Once more she felt as if she were liquid and not solid. She felt supple and fluent and light. As if she were at one with the whole world around her.

"Oh, here we are." Said Hannah, laughing.

"Thank goodness for that." Said Greg as he placed his bag on the grass and stretched his back. "I'm glad that went well. Can we have a break please before we try that again?"

Arianne laughed. "That was amazing, Gran and Grandad. Wait till I tell mum."

"I'm not sure if this will please or horrify your mother Arianne. We will have to wait and see. Meanwhile, I think we need to get on with our picnic and then get back home for tea and maybe text mum again to make sure it's all right for you to stay over. What's the time Greg?"

"It's just twelve thirty. A perfect time for a picnic."

29

GOING SOLO

I didn't need the alarm telling me it was five am. Sleep had not found me at all, apart from a few minutes when I had a nightmare. A dream about swimming in an outdoor pool and then suddenly the water all draining away. Me still swimming as if in treacle and waking up with a pool of sweat on my chest.

The image in the mirror opposite my bed didn't look like me at all. Some white-faced, red-eyed ghost had slipped out of my nightmare and was staring back at me.

Placing my head in my hands, I sobbed. Why was I putting myself through this -again?

Fumbling in the drawer by my bed, I found a box of painkillers, desperate to stop the throbbing headache. I swigged two oval-shaped pills down with water from a bottle I kept by my bed—stale water. But my sandpaper mouth didn't take much notice. More water poured down my dry throat. I must stay hydrated.

I picked up my mobile phone and began a text message to

say I'd decided to cancel. Then put the phone back down again as all the water I'd drunk gurgled up from my stomach. It went back down again, leaving a sour taste in my mouth.

I can't cancel. I was aware of all those people who'd help organize the event. People had put a great deal of effort into hiring the building, the chairs, and the floral displays. The volunteers -working for nothing. The money mum had given me for the entry fee and my overheads–of which there were so many.

My stomach churned once more. I heaved and ran to the bathroom just as an explosion of vomit hit the toilet pan.

I was red-faced and sweating—my head still thumping.

I remembered mum saying that dry toast and a cup of tea can help calm a nervous stomach. I headed downstairs and put two slices in the toaster and made myself half a cup of coffee. Then took another painkiller, thinking I'd probably sent the other two tablets down the toilet along with all that water.

The itinerary was on the worktop. I went through it for the third time while waiting for the toast to pop up.

No make-up, it said. The make-up artist will sort us all out before our performance. How can I travel on the underground - my red eyes exposed to thousands of people? I needed make-up. More tears fell as I dragged my aching, weary body up the stairs to my bedroom.

I glanced at my beautiful gown, hanging on the wardrobe door. I'd never worn a dress like that -ever. The satin skirt felt soft to my trembling fingertips.

I made a vow that I would get through this day somehow– I've done it before, and I can do it again.

The toast and coffee appeared to have helped settle my nervous stomach. I needed to get a move on and pack my gear, but my hands were shaking so much I had to keep folding my clothes. I got annoyed with myself. Why can't I fold things neatly? Mum does. The more I tried, the worse it got. My clothes ended up in a tangled pile in my suitcase. I tipped the pile out onto the bed and tried once more.

I wanted to leave my gown until the last minute, so I didn't crease it. Then I remembered the girls in 'dress' would steam out any imperfections. They always did a grand job of making me look my best. I had forgotten. I was thinking I was brain dead.

Butterflies gathered in my stomach. What if my memory failed me? What if my mind went blank? I imagined myself standing on the stage motionless and the audience booing. My hands shook again.

After packing, I left the suitcase lid open for the final bits and pieces that I needed.

Off for a quick shower and get dressed. A glance at the clock told me the taxi would soon be here.

I scanned my bedroom and checked my suitcase—nothing left on the dressing table. Everything I needed was packed. Pills, water bottle in my small bag. Handbag.

I managed to carry everything at once down the stairs and waited by the front door until I heard the honk from the taxi.

Just in-time -thank goodness.

"We usually charge extra for luggage like yours, miss."

I didn't answer. I had no answer. I was already drained of any energy I thought I might be able to muster.

The taxi driver must have taken pity on this ashen-faced, swollen eyed monster.

"Just this once, but remember next time please, to let us know you'll have a lot of heavy luggage."

I managed a nod and sat in the rear seat. I wanted to sleep. I wanted to be transported off to some desert island where I could live happily ever after. I knew this would not happen.

I took Mum's card out of my pocket and read it.

'Good luck on your special day. Sorry, I can't make it, but work won't let me have any time off as we're short-staffed here at the prison, as usual. I will be thinking of you. Love Mum xx' There was a little heart shape and a smiley face.

I kissed the card and put it back in my pocket. In a way, I was glad mum was not going to be there. What if it all went wrong? What if I couldn't perform? What if I forgot something? Those thoughts sent my mind rummaging through all my luggage to make sure I'd remembered to pack everything. My stomach went back up into my mouth. I clasped my hand over my lips and took some deep breaths.

We arrived at the railway station.

"Shall I help you with your luggage onto the train, Miss?"

"Yes, I would be so very grateful if you could do that."

I had completely forgotten how I would get four pieces of luggage onto the underground train. I was so used to mum helping me. Now I was on my own for the first time.

The train arrived at the underground station. The taxi driver and two passengers helped me with my luggage.

"Thank you."

"You're very welcome."

I stood up all the way—only a few stops. I needed to guard my luggage. I was not going to let it out of my sight for one moment.

The train stopped. I lurched forward, feeling week again. All the arrows on the platform seemed to point to where I was going. As if they were telling me–this way–you can't get out of it now, young lady.

I waved at a platform attendant who immediately understood that I needed a trolley and some assistance. Help was at hand, thank goodness.

A second taxi ride. This driver did not complain about the amount of luggage I had.

Then we arrive at the venue.

More people at the entrance to help. Things were, at last, getting easy. I made my way to the make-up room. The make-up artist had better be good. I would need as much help as I could to sort out this ashen face and red eyes-maybe plastic surgery wouldn't go amiss.

The girl was very welcoming. She sat me down and began with my hair. Brushing it and smoothing it down my back helped calm my nerves.

"Have you been doing this a long time?" she asked.

"Yes, a few years, but it doesn't get easier."

Then she began with my make-up. She took some false eyelashes from their box and was about to place one on my upper right eyelid when suddenly the butterflies in my stomach took over, and I needed the bathroom post haste.

I ran and found the sink, but the vomit did not appear. I looked in the mirror at my still pale face, and the one eyelash had glued my lids together. I staggered back to the make-up room.

"We can soon sort this out. No worries."

She sorted the eyelashes out. And the lipstick and rouge. I looked like a human being once more. I was feeling a little better too.

Some plain biscuits and a cup of coffee went down well.

The dress lady came in with my gown and helped me with it.

Everything was going well. Butterflies were kept to a minimum. Hands no longer shaking.

It was 5 pm-it had been twelve hours. I made my way down the long corridor.

I waited in the wings for my turn. The usher annoyingly held his arm out in front of me. Then he told me he would lift three fingers. He would then say and indicate three, two, one, and I was to walk out onto the stage in front of what seemed to me to be millions of people. Millions of eyes focussed on only me.

My legs turned to jelly just as the usher lifted his arm.

Three fingers went out.

He counted them.

"Three, two, one," and almost pushed me to get me going.

My legs worked-just. I walked out and stood on the mark on the stage. I could hear the orchestra fidgeting behind me. I hoped the orchestra was ready. I could hear my heart thumping as if it was about to leave my chest, and I felt sweat appear on my forehead.

I looked across and nodded at the conductor. He nodded back and lifted his arm. Vomit rose from my stomach as I placed my violin under my chin and made myself comfortable with my beloved instrument.

I shook my head to get my long hair off my face, and then stood upright, took a deep breath, told myself to relax. I placed my fingers on my instrument, my bow came down across the strings, and I was immediately transported to paradise.

I soared above the skies and into The Hall of The Mountain King. Then I was tossed among the waves in Fingal's Cave. Finally, I joined The Carnival of The Animals and glided along with The Swan.

I was exhausted and exhilarated simultaneously.

I concluded my three pieces and slowly lowered my violng and bow to my side. There was an eerie silence within the auditorium. The words of my tutor flashed through my mind.

"If there is complete silence at the end of your performance, before the audience begins to applaud, it will be because they love you."

I waited. The silence seemed to last for hours. A blush began to rise as my mind told me of all the things the audience did not like about me and my violin. Then a roar and the audience rose to its feet as one. The applause was deafening. I bowed to my left, my right, to the orchestra and conductor, then back to the middle again. I was elated. It was the best performance of my entire life.

30

BEGGARS CAN'T BE CHOOSERS

"Are you ready yet?"

"Won't be long."

Sally picked up the dog lead, her coat and placed her walking boots by the door. She stood at the bottom of the stairs, listening for movement. There was none. No good calling out again or shouting as this always had the opposite effect. She decided to wash the breakfast dishes.

The dog sat by the front door in anticipation. Sally stroked her and told her it wouldn't be that long before they were off on their early morning walk.

Sally had bounced out of bed and looked out the window at the morning mist. Perfect weather for a walk. She loved the days when the sun peeped through the mist. It was neither too hot for her nor her dog Mitsy. She imagined herself walking through the woods and then out into the meadow. Watching the butterflies, listening to the Skylarks - rare in these parts, she thought. She imagined Mitsy bouncing through the long grass filled with wildflowers. Sally wondered what the sky would look like and if there would be any puffy white clouds, she could photograph. Would she see any Buzzards today? She hoped they could pass by the lake too and see if the geese were still there.

"How long will you be?"

"Not long now. Just putting my socks on."

Socks, Sally thought. Is that as far as he's got? Putting his socks on. She sighed and stroked Mitsy again.

Sally dried the dishes and put them all away.

Again, she went to the bottom of the stairs to listen for 'getting ready' noises. There was a slight sound, a shuffle, but that was it. Better keep quiet so as not to make him cross, she thought.

Sally tidied up the magazines in the rack. Then she straightened the cushions and covers on the sofa and armchairs. She might as well empty the bins while she was at it and see if any dog poo needed clearing up while she was up in the garden.

Sally looked at her little vegetable plot. Everything growing well. She felt the washing as she walked down the garden. Not dry yet. She looked up at the bedroom window and saw the shape of David moving about. Ah, not long now, she thought.

Sally made herself another cup of tea and gave Mitsy a pat.

"Will you be long, darling?"

"Nearly ready." Came the reply from upstairs.

Sally watched the early morning news and sipped her tea. From time to time looking out the lounge window at the Blackbirds, Pigeons and Sparrows. She turned the tv off and straightened the cushions once more.

"Shall I unlock the car doors and put our bits in there? "She thought these words might hurry David along.

"I'll do it. I'll be down in a minute."

Sally put the car keys back on the sideboard. Then she tidied up the small stack of dog towels and blankets she'd got ready for the car. She put Mitsy's collar on and stroked Mitsy's back.

"Not long now, Mitsypoo. We'll soon be on our way and you can enjoy your lovely walkies, can't you." Mitsy wagged her tail in reply.

Sally stood at the bottom of the stairs again, wondering whether to tell David to get a move on or not.

"Are you nearly ready, David? The times getting on."

"I know. I'm trying my best. I'll only be a few more minutes."

"Shall I put Mitsy in the car?"

"If you like, but I won't be long, and she might get too hot or distressed and I don't want you leaving the car unlocked while we're still in the house."

"Okay David. Please hurry up we've been waiting ages."

"I'm doing my best." Shouted David.

Sally tickled Mitsy behind her ear. Mitsy panted and then wagged her tail.

"I know Mitsy, you've been waiting ages. So, have I. Why can't he get up early like he promised? Why can't he get a move on when he knows we all want to go out for the day?"

David slowly descended the stairs, entered the kitchen and went over to make himself a cup of tea.

"Haven't you had enough cups of tea this morning? You'll be wanting to stop for a pee all the time while we are out."

"I've only had two cups. Anyway, I need my breakfast before we go."

"Haven't you had your breakfast yet?"

"No. What's the rush. We've got all day, haven't we?"

Sally looked at the clock, it was nearly eleven and she'd been up since six. She went into the lounge and straightened the magazines, cushions, covers and the television controls. Then she went up the garden and felt the washing again. It was nearly dry, but not worth bringing in just yet as they were about to go out.

David sat watching the news channel as he ate his cornflakes.

"Look at all this rubbish they keep putting out here on the news."

"Can we get a move on please David? Never mind the news and the telly."

"I'm going as fast as I can."

David put his cereal bowl in the sink.

"Do you know where my walking boots are, Sally?"

"You probably left them in the shed at the bottom of the garden."

"Ah, yes, I remember." David ambled down the garden admiring the flowers, shrubs and vegetable patch. He collected his walking boots from the shed and sat on the sofa, sorting out the laces.

Sally went into the bathroom and straightened the towels, turned off the dripping tap and put the toilet seat lid back down. Then she straightened the pictures on the mantelshelf.

"Where are the car keys, Sally?"

"Where you left them."

"I can't see them anywhere."

"On the sideboard."

"Nope."

Sally walked over to the sideboard, put her hand into the little dish in the centre, pulled out the car keys and plonked them in David's hand.

"Have you got everything ready Sally? Bag, shoes, dog blankets and towels? Do we need to take water and any fruit or sannys to eat?"

"I've done my water and a bottle for Mitsy."

"Where's my water bottle?"

"Where you left it."

"Where's that?"

Sally opened a kitchen cupboard, took out a water bottle and banged it on the kitchen counter.

"I'll open the car and put Mitsy in."

"Okay, won't be a minute. Just got to put my boots on, fill my water bottle and go to the toilet."

Sally pulled the front door open, unlocked the car doors and placed all the bits and pieces she thought were necessary for the walking trip onto the rear seat. Then she put Mitsy in the car.

"Come on girlie, time for your walkies now."

Mitsy eagerly jumped into the back of the car and Sally pushed the rear door down.

"Are you ready, David?"

"Coming in a minute. Have we got everything? Is Mitsy in the car?"

"Yes everything, including Mitsy is in the car. Shall I get in?"

"Okay. I'll be two seconds."

Sally sat in the car and wiped the inside of the windows with a cloth. She turned and stroked Mitsy.

David came out of the house and went back in again.

"I've forgotten the car keys." He smiled at Sally.

"I've got them here." Sally held up the car keys and jingled them.

David sat in the driver's seat and gave an enormous sigh.

"Gosh, this is hard work getting ready to go for a walk in the country."

Sally did not answer.

"Have you locked the front door?"

"No."

David got out of the car and went to lock the front door.

"Where are the car keys?"

Sally rattled the keys in front of David's nose.

"Right, we're off at last, Mitsy. Are you going to enjoy your little walkies today, then? Won't it be fun?"

Sally looked at the car clock -it was nearly twelve noon and she had to be back to pick up the grand kids by two. She sighed. Never mind, it would still be nice just to see some green grass, wildflowers and maybe the lake, if everything went well and if they had time. Beggars can't be choosers, she thought.

31

LAURA'S LONG DISTANCE LORRIES

"Hello. Is that Mr. Hammond? Barry Hammond?"

"Yeah."

"Ah, Mr. Hammond, It's Laura from Laura's Long-Distance Lorries. Can I call you Barry, Mr. Hammond?"

"Yeah."

"Ah, well, um Barry, I just received your application form this morning to join our marvelous team of drivers. I must say you've had an impressive amount of experience according to your cv. Been driving lorries for ten years, I understand. That's just what I'm looking for here at Laura's Long-Distance Lorries. Someone with considerable expertize. Is there anything you would like to ask me about the job?"

"No, don't think so. I've had that much driving work, it's water off a duck's back, really."

"Yes, I quite agree Mr. Hammond, Barry. Water off a duck's back. Just one thing here that you ought to know. We've fully equipped all our lorries for sleeping in overnight. Now some companies will not allow this and then you have to find a motel or somewhere to stay before you collect your return haulage. We, on the other hand, don't mind this at all. I see from your application form that you were hoping to sleep in the lorry accommodation overnight. So that will be fine with me."

"Yeah."

"Now Barry, you omitted to answer one question."

"It's a long paper -more like a book than an application form."

"Yes, I do agree there, Barry," Laura chuckled.

"I don't suppose you deliberately let the question go. After all, it is well hidden among all the other questions a bit. It's on page twelve, part B, section three. You've filled everything else in nicely."

"Yeah, took me a while -half a day or more."

"Yes, Barry I quite understand but we do like to be thorough here at Laura's Long-Distance Lorries. We do like to be confident with whom we are employing as drivers. It's a responsible job, you know. I'm sure you're the perfect candidate. You just need to answer this one question."

"Yeah."

"I was hoping you could start on Monday as we are so short of men at the moment. Look, Barry, I've got a driver who'll be in your area later today. I'm going to send him over with the form. Can I leave it with you? Just answer that question and you can start on Monday."

"Yeah. I'll be at home. No-where else to go at the moment."

"Lovely, really lovely. My driver can collect it again tomorrow when he's back out there with another delivery and we can get you sorted to begin work with this amazing company next week. Does that sound great, Barry?"

"Yeah. Great."

\#

"Is that Mr. Hammond, Barry?"

"Yeah."

"Look, sorry Barry but I've got your application form back here from the driver and you've still not filled in question B, part three on page twelve. It's a very important question. I know it's tucked away among all the others, but it really does need answering. It's a police thing, you know. Nothing to do with me."

"I looked through the paper, to be quite honest, but couldn't find what to answer. It looked to me as if I'd done it all, anyway."

"Yes, Barry, I know it can be confusing. You're not the first. But I really do need to have this part filled in with your own handwriting. I was looking forward to you starting with your first delivery on Monday. What if I ask you to come into the office tomorrow morning and we can go over the form together and make sure I haven't missed anything and neither have you? I can show you the question then."

"Yeah, okay."

"Mid-morning?"

"Fine."

\#

"Ah Jack. While you're here can you look at this form from Barry Hammond? I'm hoping he can start as a new driver on Monday, but he hasn't filled in all the bits. Look here. Is it me or not? He hasn't filled it in, has he? Though he thought he had."

"No Laura, you're right. You're not dreaming. Easily done with those forms. Why don't you make them shorter? I know I hated filling all mine in. It got so boring after a while. That's probably what happened here with this bloke."

"I expect you're right, Jack. Yes, I'll see if I can cut out some of the questions in future. Thank you. Thanks for your help."

"No problem Laura."

\#

"Ah Mr. Hammond, Barry. Pleased to meet you face to face at last. Please take a seat. How are you today?"

"Fine. Thanks."

"Good. Would you like a coffee?"

"No thanks. Don't want to be too long today, I need to get some stuff sorted out if I'm beginning here on Monday."

"Ah, yes, I quite understand. I'm really looking forward to you starting work with us next week. Look, here are the keys to your lorry and your logbook." Laura jingled the keys and lay them back on top of the blue logbook.

"Now here's the form. Page twelve, question B, part three. Have you ever been convicted of a firearms offence?"

Barry suddenly stood up. The chair made a grating noise as he forced it back across the wooden floor.

"Barry? What's up? What are you doing?"

"Nothing Miss Laura of Laura's Long-Distance Lorries. Nothing at all. You're the one who's going to be doing something, and that is to open the safe right now. If not, I'll blast your head right off with this firearm. And the answer to your question is, yes, I have been convicted of firearms offences. Three, to be precise. But this time I'm going to get away with it. OPEN THE SAFE!"

Laura fumbled in the drawer for the key. Kneeled down by her desk and placed the key in a small concealed lock and lifted the floorboard. Then she turned the dial and opened the safe door, revealing wads of notes. She stepped back up against the wall. Her face ashen.

Just as Barry was putting the money into a bag Jack came in through the door. Laura screamed. There were two shots, hardly a second between them. Two people lay on the floor. No movement. Barry put the gun and the money in the bag and went over to the desk.

"Thanks for the keys but I won't be starting work on Monday. I'll be miles away, kipping in my lorry out in the sticks."

32

THE NUN'S STORY

Right from the start the room appeared claustrophobic. It made me more nervous than usual. White ceiling. Green walls. Everything else brown. Bodies everywhere.

I pushed myself into a space on the dark wood bench. Its high back more reminiscent of a church pew than a waiting room. It dug into my shoulder blades and the back of my head annoying the hell out of me. A dentist's ploy to make you so uncomfortable you do not fill up his waiting room on emergency treatment only mornings.

The bench seats took up three of the four walls. Every inch filled. Two people standing in the corner near a sad looking green shrub. A messy pile of magazines on a small table near the entrance.

I was squished between a child aged about eight and an elderly gentleman who continuously cleared his throat and fiddled with his glasses. The young girl swinging her legs making her body rock with each movement. A bony shoulder pushing against mine in rhythm to each swing. Hands either side of her knees holding onto the wooden seat which gave me even less room. I did not want to sit on her fingers and squash them flat. I was now at least a stone heavier than my usual weight.

The old man's arm irritatingly banged mine each time he shoved his glasses back up his nose.

I had no idea where I was in the queue that Saturday morning. Was it a case of the one nearest the door going in first? Or did you have to make a mental note of who was in the room before you. I'd never been any good at remembering names or faces.

At nine thirty a nurse came out holding a file. She called out a name.

"Anderson." She said as she looked around at the blank faces.

Eyes glanced left and right. No-one moved.

She looked at the file again. "Anderson." She said louder.

A skinny teenager sitting in the corner by the door began to move slowly, reluctantly.

The nurse hastened her forward.

Eyes followed the girl as she entered the dentist's surgery. Bottoms shimmied along the bench now each of us had more room to move. I studied the distorted bodies sitting opposite me. Tall and thin as if a pair of heavy bookends had forced them together.

Two minutes later the skinny teenager was back. Bottoms shuffled along again to make a slot for her slender frame.

The nurse, carrying another file, came out behind the thin girl.

"Lee, Law, Lowee? Anyone here Chinese?"

Heads turned. No Chinese people as far as anyone could see.

"Lau?" A very English looking lady rose to her feet. "Lau. My husband is from China."

I'm sure the nurse's complexion reddened slightly. A couple of people hung their heads as if in shame the faux pas might be theirs. Others tried to turn away and hide their embarrassed faces.

An expanding torso or someone new instantly filled the empty spaces left by people entering the dentist's surgery.

The surgery door opened once more. The nurse stepped forward, file in hand. She lifted her head to call a name. The skinny teenager stood up and hurried across the room toward the nurse.

"Has the dentist forgotten me?" she tried to ask, but it appeared the local anesthetic had taken hold. Her lips and tongue no longer working properly. "Ath the thenthith thorgogen ge?"

The nurse tutted and quickly waved her into the surgery. A few soft chuckles echoed around the room. A change from having to stare at somber looking faces.

Everyone on my bench, once more, did the Saturday morning dentist shuffle.

I began wondering whether I would be there all day and wish I'd bought a book with me. I tried to read the newspaper held by the man opposite me -RAID ON JEWELERS' SHOP was all I could make out from that distance. I'd left my glasses at home - again. I spent the next five minutes imagining robbers with guns holding up jewelers in the town center.

The entrance door groaning as it opened a few inches interrupted my daydreaming. All heads turned as a ray of sunshine crept in and lit up the dowdy shrub in the corner. Three nuns nervously stepped inside and carefully closed the door behind them. Their long blue habits finishing just above what my mother often called 'sensible shoes.' Shiny and black. Not like mine that had never seen a tin of polish since the day I bought them. It always intrigued me how anyone could sit and shine their shoes to such a high degree. A boring task I gave up as soon as I left school and was no longer subjected to the daily inspection of clothes and kit.

Is it usual for nuns to visit a dentist, I pondered? It appears so on this occasion.

One sister stood looking at the floor, her veil hiding most of her face. She was holding her chin. Her rising and falling shoulders showing hushed sobbing. A half silent sort of -oh my gosh circumnavigated the waiting room.

People fidgeted, nervous. No-one had seen a nun in a dentist surgery before let alone three.

The tallest nun ushered the crying nun nearer the surgery door. They stood there, in the center of the square formed by the brown wooden benches. No-one offered them a seat.

Are you supposed to give up your seat for a sister or is it just pregnant women and the elderly? No-one seemed to know. No-one bothered anyway.

The nurse came out with another patient and another file. She sighed and looked at the three nuns.

"You'll have to come in." The nurse beckoned with her hand.

The three nuns disappeared into the surgery.

Behind the closed-door voices grew louder. A male voice -the dentist. A female voice arguing back -a nun. Do nuns shout or argue? I thought they were peace-loving people.

Then loud crying. The surgery door opened again.

The nuns hurried out in their long blue gowns and wide white veils. Dissatisfaction written across their faces. Excruciating pain written across the face of the smaller nun. She lifted her head and exposed the enormous lump on the side of her jaw. Her cheeks wet with tears.

I heard sympathetic gasps. Everyone aware of the agony she must be in. Glad it was someone else's tooth and not theirs.

The two nuns hugged the smaller one while pleading with the nurse to do something. As the surgery door opened the dentist rushed out.

"I cannot help you. I simply cannot help you. I keep telling you. Go away." He shouted.

The nun with the lump began wailing. Everyone in the room expressed their unease at viewing such a spectacle.

A sobbing nun. An angry dentist. Maybe I'd somehow entered a parallel universe this Saturday.

My toothache seemed to have suddenly disappeared.

I stood up which left a space in which two people could easily have sat down. On the bus home I promised to make an appointment at a new surgery the following Monday.

ABOUT THE AUTHOR

Barbara Burgess began writing her first novel at about the age of ten. It was a story about how a dog rescued a little boy. Barbara did not have a clue about publishing and she sent her written copy off to some publishers. She had a very nice letter back saying that they rarely read unsolicited manuscripts but had read hers. They said it had a good beginning and a good ending.

At a very young age Barbara also had some poems printed in the local newspapers.

Barbara has enjoyed writing poetry, short stories and self help books for many years now. She currently has written about sixteen books.

Barbara continues to write short stories, songs, and poems and is also continues with her art and playing the piano.

facebook.com/barbaraburgesspsychicmedium

ALSO BY BARBARA BURGESS

Afternoon Tea. To Make You Laugh, To Make You Cry, My Poetry

Coffee? Don't Mind If I Do. My Poetry, Volume Two

A Funny Thing Happened On My Way to the Church

You will find more of Barbara's works at Amazon.com and Amazon.co.uk

SONGWRITING

I have been writing poetry since I was about ten years of age. I have had some poems published in local newspapers, also from a very early age.

I have self published, under my publishing name - Crowfoot Publishing - two books of my poetry - Afternoon Tea, To Make You Laugh, To Make You Cry, My Poetry and Coffee? Don't Mind If I do, My Poetry Volume Two.

Afternoon Tea was written because we, as a family, often had afternoon tea together.

Coffee? Was written because my husband Richard used to drink gallons of the stuff and our younger daughter, Selena also loves to drink coffee.

My mother had a lovely voice. She was always singing. We also watched films and tv shows that contained music and songs and we listened to songs on the radio. My dad bought a record player and we started to listen to records. Mum had Bolero which had a scratch halfway through the first side of the record and you had to move the needle and miss a bit of the music. Then you had to turn the record over to listen to the rest of the piece. We also had 1812 Overture on a black vinyl record. I loved those pieces.

I began playing the piano and the organ at about age sixteen or maybe younger. I was told I was very good but when it came to exams I was petrified and so stopped going to lessons.

It wasn't until I took the Modern Energy Art and Art Therapy course with Silvia Hartmann in 2019 that I began to rekindle my love of music. As part of the course one had to write a song.

About that time I was with our granddaughter Skye and younger daughter Selena and husband Richard at a park. We went on the miniature railway. This made me think of a song - Train To Nowhere. It just came into my head, out of the blue.

My friend and GoE Trainer Sandra Hillawi wrote songs and poems and told me that one of her songs had got into the finals of a competition. I looked around for song and poetry competitions and found The John Lennon Song Contest. I entered my song but heard nothing back about whether or not I had won. The winners and runners-up won equipment like guitars and speakers and such like.

Then another friend of mine on social media, Wendy Fry, posted something about 'I woke up this morning.' I replied to the post that it sounded like a song and Wendy challenged me to write one. This I did. I wrote - I Woke Up One Morning.'

I then found The U K Songwriting Contest on Google and entered both these songs, my very first, and was totally amazed that I got Four Stars, Commended for the lyrics of Train To Nowhere and Three Stars for the version with the melody.

I received Four Stars, Commended for, 'I Woke ~Up One Morning' lyrics and Three Stars for the song with the melody. I was over the moon! It spurred me on and I continued to write more songs.

Oh My Love - gained Five Stars, Commended. This song

was for a challenge where you write new words to the tune of Paul McCartney's 'Yesterday'.

Forever gained Five Stars, Commended in the lyrics section, Four Stars Commended in the Love songs Section. Three Stars and Five Stars Commended in other sections.

'Lover's Duette', 'From Heaven I'll Watch Over You', 'Standing On My Own Two Feet' and 'Love Is The Greatest Gift Of All' gained SEMI FINALS STATUS with Five Stars, Commended. A great achievement for my very first attempts at song writing. I am so thrilled. The Semi Finalist songs also won several other awards.

Three more songs, 'Because I've Got You', 'Boom', and Let Me Mend Your Broken Heart', also won several Star Awards and Commended.

A thrilling experience to say the least.

I continue to write songs and poems.

Here is a link to my Sound Cloud page:

Sound Cloud

BARBARA'S PERSONAL AND PROFESSIONAL QUALIFICATIONS

Songwriting with The Songwriting Academy
    Reiki and Seichem Master
    Certificate of Clairvoyance
    Angel Card Reader
    Mediumship
    Medical Intuitive
    Animal Healer
    Crystal Healing
    Spiritual Healing
    A Member of The Guild of Energists
    Freeway CER (similar to EFT)
    EFT - Emotional Freedom Technique
    Tapas Acupressure Technique (TAT)
    Guild of Energists (GoE) Money
    GoE Star Matrix Master
    GoE Modern Energy Art Master and Modern Energy Art Therapy

Barbara's Personal and Professional Qualifications

GoE Energy Symbols Master
EMO - Emotional Transformation now known as EmoFree

CONTACT

Barbara Burgess
    website - www.barbaraburgess.co.uk
    email - hello@barbaraburgess.co.uk

Printed in Great Britain
by Amazon